IVY LEE'S RUE

Valerie D. Wade

Dedication

I dedicate this book to all the Ivy Lee's in our lives struggling with mental health challenges. Continue to navigate through life and reclaim normalcy and a sense of clarity that you deserve.

We see you, we hear you, we love you, and feel your pain.

Contents

Prologue

Anson County

Ivy Lee and Mabel strolled in the blaring heat of the summer sun. They picked up groceries from the general store with the list their Mother, Tommie made. Her cryptic shopping list, because of her lack of education, showed letters missing from about every word. The two sisters traveled this dusty country road many times. Flowering dogwood trees permeated the air and lined the path with white and pale-yellow blooms, creating a full bouquet.

They once loved this routine, but since they reached their teens, they garnered unwanted stares from boys and men. Every time they went into town, they ran into a group of older boys. It was the same group of rude, rowdy boys they tried to ignore. Ivy Lee liked the attention, but Mabel knew not all attention was good. Mabel, tasked with keeping Ivy Lee focused on their chore, was three years older than Ivy Lee. She didn't seek their attention; if Ivy Lee got into trouble, they both were in trouble.

Ivy Lee was a curious wanderer. She was a happy child, not quite a teenager. Her body developed at age nine, appearing older than other girls her age. She was also quite immature for her age, and distracted by boys. Tommie wouldn't let Ivy Lee go anywhere without Mabel or their older brother, Frank. Mabel knew Ivy Lee couldn't understand the consequences.

When they arrived back at home, Tommie, with a furrowed brow, was standing in the doorway, tapping her foot. They hurried their gait because they knew it was much too long.

"What took you two so long? It shouldn't have taken that long!"

Ivy Lee turned her gaze away from Mabel's angry stare as she stomped into the house. Mabel let the door slam into Ivy Lee's face. Tommie swatted Ivy Lee on her behind as she tried to explain.

"Mabel tried to leave me. I'm sorry, Mama."

"It wasn't me, Mama! She was taking her time, and I didn't want to leave her behind. The next time I'll go by myself!" She pushed past Ivy Lee, heading to set the table.

Although living with meager means, dinner was an important gathering time for the Harris family. Mabel unfolded the lace-worn tablecloth and spread it across the scratched oak table. It was Ivy Lee's job. Mabel followed her around, rearranging the forks and mason jar glasses. She was used to Mabel's annoying habit and ignored her.

After they were done, they hurried outside. Frank was swaying on the makeshift swing behind the house. Frank, being the only boy, ignored the regular banter between his sisters, never getting between them. Sometimes, he would take up for Ivy Lee when he thought Mabel was getting too bossy.

"Mabel, you're jealous I'm getting more attention than you." Ivy Lee shouted.

"I'm not jealous. You're a silly little girl, and you don't understand. Watch out for those boys!"

Frank didn't see Mabel standing near the swing. He dreamed of becoming a pilot. The roar of a plane's engine overhead distracted him. His outstretched legs hit her straight in the stomach, knocking her backward. She came close to hitting her head and scraped her knuckles on the gravel beneath the swing.

"Mama!" Ivy Lee screamed.

Frank leaped out of the swing, grabbing Mabel by the arm. He helped her up and brushed the dirt and grass from her dress. "I'm sorry, I didn't see you!"

Mabel never liked to show weakness, so she blinked away the tears. Noticing the torn hem at the bottom of her favorite blue dress, she limped back to the house. Throwing Frank an angry glance, she made an exaggerated hobble up the steps.

She ain't hurt bad, Frank thought as he returned to swinging. Even with the way Mabel treated Ivy Lee, she rushed behind Tommie, taking Mabel's other arm to help guide her into the house.

Chapter 1

A New Blessing

It was clear Tommie missed Mabel's help while she was away, even though Ivy Lee helped as much as she could. She was so glad her Mother let her stay for a few weeks with Daddy's sister in Charlotte before Mabel returned home. Tommie told Ivy Lee she would have a little brother or sister. Ivy Lee never noticed her mother was expecting. Their father pulled out the old cradle, and Tommie gathered some clothes she made and others the Green family gave her. Ivy Lee was so excited. She didn't care whether it was a brother or sister. She loved babies and couldn't wait.

When Ivy Lee returned from Charlotte, she was excited to meet her new little sister, Georgia. She was beautiful, like a little doll with hazel eyes. Ivy Lee marveled at her small size and eye color. Her hair was fine, sandy, and straight, and she had a light complexion. She couldn't wait to hold her, but now bossy Mabel was back; She felt she wouldn't get the chance. Mabel seemed happier than before Ivy Lee left for Charlotte.

Ivy Lee stared down at Georgia in the knotty walnut crib, swaddled on her back in a pink blanket with both arms up. Her chubby fingers curled into little fists. Her hair outlined her forehead as if painted on. Ivy Lee adored her. She couldn't stay away.

Mabel ran to tell Tommie she was hovering over Georgia again. Tommie, tired from work, too exhausted to engage Mabel, and waved her away.

"Now Mabel, let dat chile be. You know she loves her." Mabel, fuming, left the kitchen and stood watching Ivy Lee before Tommie called for Ivy Lee's help with dinner.

Mabel spends a lot of time with her. Ivy Lee pouted as she put away groceries Tommie brought home. She glanced into the living room, seeing Mabel coo and cradle Georgia.

Tommie let Ivy Lee peel the potatoes while the water was boiling for mashed potatoes. The aroma of fried chicken permeated the modest house. Ivy Lee enjoyed cooking. She mastered Tommie's sweet potato pies. She complimented Ivy Lee's cooking and told her she looked forward to Ivy Lee taking over one day. Ivy Lee would make her way to the kitchen every chance she got to shadow her Mother. Tommie let her take over so she could rest her swollen feet and ankles, supporting her full-figured frame. She was big-boned, dark-skinned, and stood six feet tall. An attractive woman, but she appeared weary, bags and dark circles under her eyes now. She would arrive home at dusk each evening stiff and exhausted, creeping over to her chair.

Ivy Lee was a daddy's girl. Johnny, a sharecropper, arrived home tired from tending the fields each night. He worked their small, rented plot of fertile land to provide for the family, the only option available during this time. Their crop comprised soybeans and corn. All the tools used belonged to the landowners, including the old mule. The landowner would seek Johnny to cut down trees on other properties he owned.

Johnny stood over six feet tall. His dark brown weather worn skin deeply embedded with deep lines and wrinkles. Aged by toiling in the torrid heat of the south. As a young boy, he labored alongside his father until leaving rural Georgia. He held odd jobs until making his way to North Carolina. His love for carpentry came from his uncle, but he appeared to have a natural ability. He loved the smell of the wood and it made him happy to create something. Johnny was so proud of the family crib he designed, which was used by all his children, and now Georgia.

5

Johnny called on Ivy Lee to sing him a song. Ivy Lee's melodious soprano notes filled the room. She waited by the door daily with Johnny's worn slippers and a cool glass of lemonade. His cigarette smoke circling his head as it balanced on his chapped bottom lip. He kicked off his tattered work boots and plopped down in the chair with an enormous sigh. This was the best part of Ivy Lee's day.

Ivy Lee fell asleep nestled in her father Johnny's lap most nights. This night was no different. He guided a sleepy Ivy Lee to her bed. Mabel hovered over Georgia while swaddling her in the crib. Tommie and Frank were already in bed. The house was so small, they could hear any cry from Georgia throughout the house, and Mabel would have Georgia in her arms before Tommie could reach her.

Johnny smiling. "Get you some sleep, girl."

"I know, Daddy, I can't stop looking at her. She is so beautiful." Mabel gave her dad a kiss on his bearded cheek. She headed towards the bedroom, glancing back at Georgia.

Baby Georgia shifted all the family's attention upon her arrival. Her crying kept the entire family awake many nights. Tommie was back working for the Green family with no break. Mabel doted on Georgia, feeding her, rocking her, and washing the endless amount of dirty diapers.

Johnny ambled over to Georgia's crib and watched her for a moment while she slept. She appeared so tiny in this crib that each of his children used; It was the little one's turn.

"Lord, bless this surprise child—bless all of them."

***

Besides singing, Ivy Lee wrote poetry. She kept her poetry hidden in an old notebook given to her by her favorite teacher, Miss Miller. Miss Miller, Ivy Lee's fifth-grade teacher, took time with a shy Ivy Lee.

Ivy Lee mustered up the courage to share her poetry with Miss Miller. All the class left the classroom, except Ivy Lee. She weaved her way through the desks left in disarray by the rushing students. Ivy Lee's thick black hair pulled back in a ponytail. Beads of sweat formed under the big bangs covering her forehead. She walked towards the front of the room. Books in arm, and carrying a wrinkled piece of paper in her trembling hand. Miss Miller stood behind the desk, overflowing with textbooks and papers, erasing the blackboard. Startled by Ivy Lee, she turned around. Ivy Lee, head down, and whispering.

"Here is a poem I wrote." Ivy Lee, never lifting her eyes from the floor.

She took the paper from Ivy Lee. "Thank you, Ivy Lee. I love poetry!" Miss Miller read each line of the poem about rain. "This is a lovely poem! I like rain too!" Miss Miller reached out and hugged a beaming Ivy Lee. She thanked Miss Miller and shoved the paper into her notebook and ran out of the classroom. Miss Miller stood there smiling. She never saw Ivy Lee this candid before.

Ivy Lee could read well. Miss Miller would often call on her to select a book and lead the class reading. She was nervous the first time she stood in front of the class. Miss Miller encouraged Ivy Lee and chastised the students, who giggled or whispered as she went to the front of the room. Ivy Lee surveyed the class and noticed two girls whispering to each other, and Miss Miller came over and put her arm around Ivy Lee to reassure her. When Ivy Lee began reading, Miss Miller stood in the back of the classroom and cleared her throat. The girls who whispered about Ivy Lee turned around, sat up in their chair, and focused their attention on her. Ivy Lee's nervousness subsided, and each time after, it became easier. Miss Miller let Ivy Lee select books to take home and gave her a special notebook. Ivy Lee only shared her poetry with Miss Miller, who made her feel important.

As usual, both Johnny and Tommie rose early each morning and left the house; Johnny to tend the fields, and Tommie to the Green family, while Mabel cared for Georgia.

Tommie worked for the Greens. Many of the household chores fell upon her children. She would work late when the Greens would have parties. On those nights, Frank, who loved sweets, waited up for the leftovers and desserts she brought home.

Before dawn, Tommie and Johnny began their daily ritual. Tommie kneeled first as she reached up to grab Johnny's calloused hand. They clasped hands as Johnny began a prayer to cover the family, calling each of them by name. Johnny led the prayer as Tommie hummed. He rose first, helping Tommie up. They shared a lingering embrace before departing for the long day ahead.

The summer brought long, sweltering days in Wadesboro. Mabel oversaw Frank and Ivy Lee, but Ivy Lee thought she was overbearing. Locked in the house with Mabel while Frank played outside and burdened with chores, she didn't get to spend much time with Georgia, whom she adored.

"Mama said to watch you. No wandering off."

Ivy Lee would retreat to her poetry when she was angry. Poetry to her was like singing. It could take her anywhere in her mind, anywhere away from mean old Mabel.

One day, I'm going to write a poem about her, Ivy Lee thought. She also knew if she wrote what she thought about her sister, she might get in big trouble. While Mabel was busy tending to Georgia, Ivy Lee quietly organized the pots and pans in the cabinets. She washed up the dishes left from breakfast and swept the kitchen; chores Mabel usually took care of.

"Mabel, I cleaned the whole kitchen because I knew you were busy. Did I do a good job?" Mabel surveyed the room. One hand on her hip and a scowl on her face. Peering into the lower kitchen cabinet, she rolled her eyes and grinned.

"Those pans go in the other cabinet. Mama won't be able to find anything now. You can set the table." Ivy Lee frowned and trudged to the drawer to pull out the silverware. *I'll have some fun. I have my ways,* she thought with a sneaky grin.

8

"Can I go play on the swings, Mabel? You can see me through the window. I promise I won't go anywhere. I've done all of my chores, and I'll even sweep the porch if you want me to." Once Mabel agreed, Ivy Lee ran out of the front door. The screen slammed behind her, and her pink-striped jumper caught the breeze. Ivy Lee picked up the ragged broom leaning against the wood-framed house and swept the porch. She noticed Mabel peeking out the window with Georgia in her arms as she swept the porch clean before she headed towards the swings. The stray hound was hanging around. It appeared now and then, but ran away when she tried to pet it. The little hound, with its nose to the ground, fixated on a scent, didn't even notice Ivy Lee. She figured he belonged to someone, and it must have gotten lost in the woods while hunting. Ivy Lee loved animals and wanted to have her own bird when she grew up. She petted any stray animal she saw, even trying to corral feral cats in the area. Tommie halted her attempts to bring home frogs she caught with Frank at the pond near their home.

Ivy Lee saw Frank down the road from the swing behind the house. Frank was standing and talking with a girl and a couple of boys. She continued swinging and daydreaming. As she swung with her eyes closed, she felt something cold and wet pressed to her knee. The stray beagle surprised her, causing her to jump off the swing. The little beagle was black, brown, and tan, and his tail was wagging. Ivy Lee bent down to touch it. She was face to face with its hazel eyes and red eyelashes. "I'm going to name you Sadie." She could hear her father state, "We don't need no flea-bitten mutt around here. I'm barely able to feed you kids; and don't be petting it." Ivy Lee rubbed it anyway. The little hound put his paws on her lap and tried to lick her face. She wished she had brought some food with her. The mysterious hound got distracted with a scent and ran back towards the woods.

"I'll save some food for you next time. It will be our secret." She kept swinging and daydreaming.

"Hey, girl!" came a familiar voice from behind Ivy Lee.

She opened her eyes, recognizing the light-skinned, hazel eyed young man as Ozias Smith from the other side of the hill. He thought he was popular with girls. She glanced around for Frank because she thought Ozias was the boy he was standing with. It seemed liked Ozais appeared out of nowhere. Ivy Lee spotted Frank distracted by Ozias' sister up the road.

Ozias, a few years older than Mabel, used to hang around trying to court her. Many of the girls liked him. Tommie warned Mabel to stay away from "dem high yeller men," but Mabel liked him. When they suddenly broke up, Ivy Lee remembers her moping around the house. Tommie told Ivy Lee Mabel went to stay with her cousins in Tampa to cheer her up and help with babysitting. A few months before, Ivy Lee overheard Tommie scolding Mabel about something.

"I came to say hi, big stockings." Shouted Ozias.

"My Daddy told you to stay away from here. I'm telling Mabel."

You don't need to call her. You didn't act this way in town at the store, did you?"

"Mabel! Mabel!"

Mabel appeared at the door holding Georgia.

"What are you doing around here? You heard what my daddy said. He'll have a talk with your folks if you come around. Ivy Lee, come in here! Stay away from me, my little sister, and this house!"

"She doesn't seem like a *little* sister to me." Winking at Ivy Lee. Ivy Lee ran towards the porch as Mabel held the door open.

Although Ivy Lee didn't realize it, Frank kept a close eye on his little sister. She would often wander off, but he didn't tell his parents or Mabel. He didn't need Ivy Lee getting in trouble. The first time it happened, he thought she was hunting for the stray dog, or chasing toads around. Every time he would question her, she would deny wandering off.

"Ivy Lee, if you keep disappearing, we will have to stay home."

"Doing what, Frank? I didn't do nothing.

10

"I have been searching for you for an hour. You scared me. Maybe you should stay home with Mabel."

"No! please don't make me. I promise I won't do it again. I don't remember." As the sun set, Frank put his arm around Ivy Lee to comfort her as they trudged home. Ivy Lee appeared confused, which puzzled him.

Chapter 2

Frank

Although Frank couldn't wait until he turned eighteen, it didn't matter. He received his notice to register for the draft well before his eighteenth birthday. He dreamed of becoming a pilot. Although Wadesboro was Frank's home, Johnny encouraged him to grab the opportunity. He drilled it into him to seek everything the world offered. "Don't get trapped here."

Johnny, a clever man with no education, was talented at drawing, but his reading skills were a challenge. He drew pictures of airplanes so detailed they appeared to fly off the page. Frank told Johnny he was going to fly one of those planes someday. When it was time to enlist, he joined the Air Force; Johnny was so proud.

The first letter Johnny received from Frank came from Lackland Air Force Base in San Antonio, Texas. Mabel read it to him and tears welled up in his eyes. He held the letter to his chest. Tommie remembered how proud Johnny was. "Dat's my boy!" She listened but stayed quiet and went back to folding laundry. Each letter brought sadness to her, but she never conveyed that to Johnny. Especially the one where he informed them of his impending deployment to Viet Nam. She was concerned about her only son. She wished they could have afforded to attend Frank's graduation from boot camp. She treasured every picture he sent. *He looks so good in his uniform,* she thought, but was still her baby boy. As Mabel read his last letter, she grew more worried. He briefly described the combat, but reassured them he was not scared and had trained for it.

***

A year later, the sharp knock on the front door on a sunny Saturday morning broke their silence, which startled them. Ivy Lee reading a book, Tommie and Mabel folding clothes, and Johnny nodding in his chair at the table. Johnny pushed his chair back and opened the door. Each inch of opening the creaky door revealed two men dressed in uniform. One was holding a large manila envelope.

"Mr. Harris?"

"Yes."

"On behalf of the United States Air Force, we regret to inform you that your son, Frank Harris, has been killed in a helicopter crash in Vietnam."

The second service man offered condolences and handed their father the manila envelope, which rattled as he handed it to Johnny. Johnny tentatively opened the lip of the envelope and reached in until his warm hand touched the cold metallic dog tags. Tears ran down his face as they heard Tommie gasp. Ivy Lee couldn't make out what they were saying. Johnny returned to the table after closing the door, pulling out the frayed picture of Frank he kept in his right shirt pocket.

"Frank's gone." He stated as he tucked the photo back in his pocket. Then he got up and embraced Tommie, doubled over with grief. He knew he couldn't console her, but he held her for the next few hours. His shirt was wet, drenched in her sorrow. Mabel and Ivy Lee prepared the meals that evening in silence. Ivy Lee couldn't cry or speak.

Ivy Lee kept thinking about how Frank protected her and took up for her when he thought Mabel was too cruel. Mabel was quiet, which was unusual for her. She knew how close they were and wondered why Ivy Lee didn't cry.

The lump in Ivy's Lee's throat seemed as large as an apple. An emptiness overcame her, but the tears never came. She was in disbelief she would never see her brother again. Later in the night, Tommie discovered Ivy Lee sobbing and curled up on Frank's old bed. Tommie didn't say a word, but rubbed Ivy Lee's back and held her until she fell asleep.

The Green family Tommie worked for gave her money so she and their father Johnny could travel to Washington, DC, for Frank's graveside service at Arlington National Cemetery. Frank was among two other soldiers who perished in the helicopter crash.

The Harris' returned with a flag they said covered Frank's casket. Johnny tried to explain the twenty-one-gun salute to them as best he could. He also brought back the shell casings, which were tied together with a red, white, and blue ribbon.

Tommie remained quiet and returned to the Green's house the next day and back to her routine. The evening found each member sitting in silence. Ivy Lee pierced the quiet with her singing of *This Little Light of Mine*. It was the first song she remembered learning, and the only song she ever heard Frank hum. "Sing my song Ivy Lee! I can't sing, but I will hum along." She obliged Frank, her protector. Ivy Lee realized that what she lost in Frank was not only a brother, but her best friend.

Chapter 3

Sisters

Ivy Lee, now in her late thirties, is full-figured. She developed before her teen years and garnered attention from men when she traveled down the street. Wide hips enhanced by the dresses she wore also accentuated her large breasts. Ivy Lee's heart-shaped face held enormous eyes with long eyelashes, and she kept her hair pressed and curled. She displayed a confidence but was naïve to the fact she suffered bouts of insanity which she seldom remembered.

Her beautiful singing voice committed a cadre of gospel songs and hymnals to memory. She radiated joy and kept a smile on her face. She loved cooking and baking and kept an immaculate home except for the ashes which fell from her extra-long cigarettes.

Ivy Lee was five years old when she exclaimed her profound faith in God. She was the first one in the Sunday school class to learn the scripture, *John 3:16. "For God so loved the world he gave his only begotten Son, whosoever believeth in him should not perish but have everlasting life."* Her Sunday school teacher, Mrs. Howard was so impressed. Soon after, she joined the children's choir.

Her husband, Willie, was a Deacon at New Mt. Sinai Baptist Church. A devoted servant to the church, spending many hours there in all capacities; custodial, gardening, and teaching Sunday School. Ivy Lee grew to resent the constant calls from church members who sought his help. He often led devotion and trained the new Deacons. Everything tickled Willie. He smiled at everyone, tipping his hat at all the women he encountered when he would go to the bank. He was the teller's favorite customer. His high-pitched laugh could echo wherever he was. When he and Ivy Lee got separated in the grocery store, she listened for Willie's laughter. He was a devoted husband with such a deep love for her, he overlooked and dealt with her mental challenges.

Willie volunteered to take care of tasks around Mabel's house, since her husband Randall spent much of his time tending to his repair shop and neglected house repairs.

Ivy Lee treated her parakeet, Sonny, like royalty. She allowed him to fly free around the apartment whenever Willie wasn't home, and catered to his every need. She never held a steady job. On good days, during segments of clarity and when she was not combative, she led several church auxiliaries. When things got bad, Willie never left her alone at church; he needed to be near to monitor her behavior. Anything could trigger her. When she heard voices in her head, she would become belligerent and spew profanity about the church.

During good times, she made many friends. She was one of the most beloved women in the church. The congregation surprising her, was one of her most treasured memories. She would reminisce this memory during those dark times.

"Surprise!" Ivy Lee startled as she entered, took the few steps down to the fellowship hall, assisted by Willie. Her eyes adjusting to the bright lights silhouetting the crowd. The head Deaconess approached Ivy Lee with what appeared to be a hat box.

"Sister Patterson, we appreciate you so much and all you do for all of our auxiliaries, and how gracious you are to share Deacon Patterson with us. This day is for you." Tears rolled down Ivy Lee's face. "Thank you so much!"

A line of church members surrounded Ivy Lee. Each reaching out to hug her. She was overwhelmed. Willie led her over to the head table decorated with a skirt that shimmered with sparkly tulle. They trimmed the entire room in balloons and crepe paper in her favorite color, royal blue. A large shiny silver wrapped box overstuffed with cards sat at the end of the head table. After the dinner was over, Ivy

Lee opened the large hat box from the Millinery shop at Hudson's Department Store downtown.

During her dark periods, those close friends and admirers would shy away. In her moments of clarity, the hurt and loneliness became much of her daily life. Her nephew Riley was the one joy she could count on. He seemed to bring out a stable calmness. No one else affected her this way.

Mabel, strong willed and bossy, bore a striking resemblance to Tommie. She was tall, very attractive, big boned, with smooth unblemished mocha skin. Her long, curly, shiny black hair, which she got from her father, stretched down to the middle of her back.

Mabel felt being the eldest was a burden having to watch out for her younger siblings. The death of Georgia left her depressed and filled with guilt. She shut her siblings out, staying in her room and crying for days. Tommie assigned her tasks where she had to interact with family and couldn't retreat to her room. As soon as she completed her tasks, she returned to her room. She replayed the events over and over. It devastated the entire family. It was then Ivy Lee first displayed signs of mental distress; her personality changed from her usual cheery disposition to being withdrawn and quiet. Her sweet nature could change in an instant.

Chapter 4

First Sunday

Since arriving in Detroit, Willie and Ivy Lee lived rent free for six months in the substantial flat above Mabel and Randall. The flat was expansive: two bedrooms, a bathroom, kitchen and a back porch overlooking a vast backyard.

Ivy Lee decorated the living room with sheer blush curtains. The flat was furnished with a full-size bed, a big brown overstuffed sofa upholstered with paisley print, matching chair, and two end tables. Mabel gave them an extra television from one bedroom in the basement. While finishing his route, Willie, a sanitation worker, found an antique red and white enamel kitchen table with collapsible leaves and a little red drawer built in the front.

"Oh, Willie! I love it. It's perfect for our kitchen."

A smile came across Willie's face as he waited for her reaction. "I knew you would like it, baby. It's in pretty good shape, too." He was pleased with his find; and something he could contribute which belonged to them.

Ivy Lee, positioned at the large kitchen sink, washed the dishes from Willie's breakfast. Willie was predictable. He wanted bacon, scrambled eggs, and toast with grape jelly every morning. It was rare for him to request any other meal. As she heard Willie driving away, the phone rang. She already knew it was Mabel because she called at the exact moment Willie left each morning. Mabel's daily intrusions, the side comments, nagging, and prying eyes were a constant annoyance for Ivy Lee. She had grown impatient and pressed Willie to search for an apartment. Mabel would call daily and pepper her with questions about her medicine regimen and how she was spending her day. She wondered how Mabel could have time to oversee her. Mabel worked full time, was a wife, Mother, and was a devout Jehovah's Witness dedicated to field work but, she still made time to keep tabs on Ivy Lee.

Before winter arrived, they moved to a nice apartment building on the west side. She felt more independent, and months passed since she felt confused. It was better for them. Ivy Lee bought a parakeet she longed for and named him Sonny. Sonny flew around the apartment, but somehow, the two communicated, and the bird retreated to his cage on command.

She loved cooking and Willie loved eating and would race home every night for a delicious home cooked meal when he was not busy with tasks at the church. Willie was thin and petite with a gigantic appetite, but he never gained weight.

"I think I'll ask Mabel if Riley can come by and stay the weekend. Ivy Lee thought.

Ivy Lee loved spending time with Riley, and he seemed to enjoy it, too. She read his favorite stories and showed poems she wrote long ago. Her love of poetry waned over the years, but she enjoyed sharing them with him. They chatted about school and all his favorite things. She read him Bible stories from the colorful illustrated children's Bible, which she kept at the apartment. He interrupted her with many questions about God, and when Ivy Lee asked him whether he wanted to be baptized, he said yes. The rest of the weekend was fun with Riley.

The church was full on the first Sunday of the month. Ivy Lee donned a big lavender hat to match her dress. She surveyed the congregation for a vacant space in the pews towards the front of the church. She recognized the elderly lead usher who limped because of one leg being shorter than the other. One hand behind her back, and wearing her starched powder blue uniform, directing parishioners with authority to "scoot down" to make more room. The frustrated usher motioned to Ivy

Lee and Riley to come towards the pew she was pointing at in the front.

After communion was served, the sermon delivered, and one last song by the choir, Pastor Jackson announced the doors of the church were open. To Ivy Lee's surprise, Riley rushed up to the front of the sanctuary and embraced Pastor Jackson. Ivy Lee smiled at Willie, who was standing at the altar with the other Deacons, nodded and summoned Riley to her. "Are you sure you want to be baptized today, baby? Have you taken Jesus into your heart?"

"Yes, Ma'am! I am ready, Auntie,"

"It makes me so happy." She embraced Riley as he ran back up to the pulpit to join the other candidates.

Willie got all of them ready. Riley was one of three children being baptized. When Pastor Jackson immersed Riley in the water, he emerged with a big grin.

After church, they returned to the apartment. Ivy Lee cooked all of Riley's favorite foods the night before.

"Auntie, can I call my mom and tell her I got baptized?"

Riley stopped by a faded framed picture on the corner table of Ivy Lee, holding an infant. He picked it up, paused, and then skipped to the telephone to call Mabel.

"Sure baby, call her." Ivy Lee said with hesitation. She wasn't sure how Mabel was going to receive the news, but Riley couldn't wait to deliver it.

He was so excited to call Mabel, but Ivy Lee dreaded Mabel's reaction as he handed the phone to her.

"Hi Sister, did you hear the news?"

"How dare you let him get baptized! You know how I feel about it!" Mabel screamed at the other end of the line. Ivy Lee, rattled by Mabel's venom coming from the receiver, didn't change her expression as Riley looked on with a big smile.

"Sister, let me explain. I didn't know he wanted to get baptized. It was a surprise to me. Can we talk about it later? I will have Willie drop him off after dinner."

"Yes! We will talk later, Ivy Lee. We will!" Mabel slammed the phone down.

Ivy Lee didn't let Riley know about the discourse in the conversation between her and Mabel. The three of them enjoyed Riley's favorite meal: baked chicken, mashed potatoes, creamed corn, collard greens, and his favorite coconut cake with pineapple cream filling. She wished she could spend more time with him, but Mabel rationed their visits, which she assumed would be less after this event.

***

Mabel tossed and turned all night and woke up enraged about Riley's baptism. She still couldn't believe Ivy Lee would let Riley get baptized without her permission. She was livid. Mabel felt Ivy Lee should have understood they would baptize Riley under the Jehovah's Witness faith.

"Riley is mine! I cannot believe her!" she screamed.

Randall grabbed Mabel's arm and led her to the sofa, hugging her while speaking in a soft tone. He tried to calm her, but she jumped up and continued to pace the room, tears welling in her eyes.

"She's not taking him from us! She's not!"

"Baby, no one is taking him. Calm down."

Mabel settled down, but she wanted to meet with Ivy Lee. Awaking at sunrise, she made the call.

I'm getting this off my mind before I go to work. We need some boundaries for Riley, she thought as she grabbed the telephone receiver.

"Hello!"

"Ivy Lee, this is Mabel. I'm coming by to talk about yesterday."

"Ok sister. What time?"

"Now! I'm coming right now!"

"Ok, I will get dressed. See you soon." Ivy Lee heard the dial tone on the other end of the phone.

An agitated Mabel arrived at Ivy Lee's apartment within ten minutes as she pierced the peaceful scene of the manicured dew-covered lawn reflecting the morning sun. She drew a deep breath and tried to calm herself as she opened the door and searched for Ivy Lee's apartment number. Her finger moving up and down the numbers so fast her eyes felt crossed. She pressed the small black button and waited.

"Hello."

"It's me Ivy Lee!"

"Ok, come on up, Sister."

Mabel snatched the gold handle as the door buzzed to release the lock. The trek up to the third floor seemed like it was endless. Ivy Lee stood in the open door with one foot out of the door on the flowered welcome mat in front of her apartment. Mabel's rapid footsteps made a sticky sound on the rubber hall runner.

"Good morning, Sister!"

"Ivy Lee. I won't be long!"

"Would you like some coffee?"

"Yes."

"Sit down at the table, I'll be right there."

Ivy Lee unplugged the percolator and sat it down on the small piece of black felt there to protect the wooden table. She poured a cup for each of them and sat down as she added two sugar cubes to her cup, followed by a small amount of Pet Milk.

Mabel drank her coffee black, as she inhaled. "Ivy Lee, we need boundaries for Riley. You should've called me to see if it was ok."

"Sister, it happened so quick. I didn't think you would mind; They baptized us around his age. He loves coming to church with me, and I can tell he loves the Lord."

"Well, I'm raising him a different way, and you know it! I was planning to have him baptized under the Jehovah's Witness faith."

"Well, I am sorry, Mabel. I didn't push him into it. It surprised me, but I think it's a wonderful thing."

After letting out a sigh, Mabel stood up over Ivy Lee. "Ivy Lee, I don't want this to happen again!"

"I'm sorry Sister. I meant no harm. You know how much I love Riley and cherish the time I spend with him."

"I know. Well, I need to get back. We'll talk soon."

"I love you, Sister."

Ivy Lee motioned to hug Mabel, but Mabel headed to the door and pulled the door shut behind her before Ivy Lee could reach it.

Mabel drove home to change clothes before going to work, still upset about Riley's baptism. "*I bet Lillian knew about this,*" she thought. Lillian, who became close with Ivy Lee when she lived upstairs, continued an ongoing tense relationship with Mabel. They were both outspoken and opinionated and Lillian was not shy about speaking up when she observed the interaction between Mabel and Ivy Lee. She witnessed Mabel being harsh with her and would let her know it every chance she got. Mabel conveyed to Lillian many times to mind her business. As she was getting out of her car, she saw Lillian standing on the screened-in porch. She thought of confronting her, but she decided against it and closed her car door and continued up the sidewalk without returning a wave from Lillian. Randall waited in the living room.

"Well, how did it go, Mabel?" He rose to greet her.

"You know how it went?" Mabel threw her purse on the couch.

"No, I don't. Tell me." He moved closer and grabbed her by the shoulders to face him.

"As usual, in her sweet innocent way, she apologized."

"Well, she was sorry."

"I don't think she was sorry at all. She said how wonderful it all was."

"Mabel, it's not the worst thing Riley could have done in his life. Be thankful he loves God, Jehovah or whomever God is to him. He's a good boy, never gives us any trouble. We're blessed to have him in our lives." Randall hugged Mabel. "I love you baby, and so does Riley. Never doubt it. He adores you."

Mabel embraced Randall. Randall could calm her down and put things in perspective.

"Thank you." She wiped away a tear. "I can't lose him, I can't."

Chapter 5

Church Anniversary

The morning of the church anniversary started a little rough for Ivy Lee. She woke up in a cold sweat immersed in the same recurring dream; cold wet mud up to her ankles, pouring rain, the faint memory of a lifeless baby, and standing over a small grave in the family graveyard back in Wadesboro. Her face covered with dried tears, stomach queasy, and her hands trembled. She refused to take those pills the doctor prescribed because they made her feel as if she were moving in slow motion. Ivy Lee called Mabel the night before to see if Riley could join them for the church's anniversary, but Mabel declined. Ivy Lee, upset, determined to make the best of the day despite her disappointment.

They arrived at church a half hour before service was about to begin. She hugged Willie as he hurried off to the Trustee room where the deacons gathered. Willie dressed in a black suit and striped black and white tie. Ivy Lee, choir robe draped over her arm, wore a polka-dotted dress, matching hat, and black patent leather purse and shoes. Once entering the choir room, she donned her robe and removed her hat and placed it on one of the wooden chairs. She checked her makeup in the wall mirror, and reapplied her bright red lipstick to her full lips. Pulling out her comb, she tidied up her hair flattened by her big church hat. Since she was early, she sat down for a few minutes and drew a deep breath. She didn't feel nervous, but her heart was pounding. She felt uneasy as she took steps from the choir room to the pulpit. Ivy Lee continued, and stood in her usual place, third from the end of the pew. She watched the pews fill with parishioners. Her solo was next, but she sat motionless wringing her perspiring hands in her lap. The choir director appeared perplexed, but remained silent signaling the choir to rise with the intro of *Pass Me Not, Oh Gentle Savior.* The organist started the introduction to the song again hoping to prompt Ivy Lee.

Willie, who was sitting in the front row with the Deacons observed her. He could tell something was wrong as she rose to her feet. Her head tilted, and she appeared to be mumbling in a low tone. Willie heard the music pause. He looked around the church. All eyes were on Ivy Lee. Ivy Lee began singing Frank's favorite song, *This Little Light of Mine.* The organist hesitated, but switched and started playing it on the piano, as the choir joined in. The rehearsed rendition wouldn't happen today. When Ivy Lee finished, she stepped down the two tattered steps of the worn red carpeted choir stand and headed straight for the center aisle of the church. She unzipped her choir robe and let it tumble to the floor as she stepped out of it and headed out the front door. The slamming of the heavy oak door echoed through the small chapel. Willie followed, gathering up Ivy Lee's robe, and the organist began the next song. By the time Willie reached Ivy Lee, he saw her across the busy street. She sat on the curb in front of an abandoned store trying to light a cigarette while her hands trembled.

"Baby, Baby what's wrong?"

Ivy Lee kept silent attempting to light her cigarette in the wind. Her eyes fixed and glazed; it didn't appear she even realized Willie was present.

Willie grabbed Ivy Lee's elbow lifting her up, while realizing her bare feet. He scooped up her shoes and guided her to their car, which was parked across the street in the lot next to the church. He noticed Ivy Lee's silence as he opened the passenger door and helped her inside. As he made his way around to the driver side, he saw Deacon Sherman heading towards their car. He raised his hand and gave a nod. Deacon Sherman appeared to understand the gesture as he headed back inside.

Ivy Lee hummed *Pass Me Not*, the song she was to have led in church. As they arrived at the parking space in front of their apartment, she appeared calmer to Willie. Her hands no longer trembled, and her gait was steadier as she slid her feet into her high heel pumps and headed towards their apartment building door.

"I cooked dinner yesterday, Willie. It's in the refrigerator. Put it in the oven on two hundred degrees. It was a wonderful service, wasn't it?" Her voice trailing off as she headed towards the bedroom, as if nothing ever happened. "I'm tired, I'm going to lie down."

"Okay Ivy Lee, get some rest." A bewildered Willie sat down waiting for his meal to warm. As he loosened his tie, the telephone rang. He rushed to grab it. His voice low so he wouldn't wake Ivy Lee.

"Hello!"

"Deacon Patterson, is everything all right? We are all worried about Sister Patterson."

"Yes, Reverend, I think she suffered another spell. She is resting now. Thank you for your concern."

"Let us know if you need anything. You know how we love Sister Patterson. If you need to miss the upcoming conference in Cincinnati, we will understand."

"I appreciate it, and I must admit I'm worried. I'll keep you posted. Thank you."

"Goodbye."

"Goodbye, I will call you tomorrow."

Willie stared down at the wooden floor until startled by Sonny fluttering in his cage. He remembered the food in the oven and raced to the kitchen to turn it off. He peeped in on Ivy Lee, who was sound asleep. *I need to call Dr. Timmons*, he thought, which he planned to do the next morning. He knew Ivy Lee didn't enjoy taking the medicine, but realized how desperately she needed it. She would have to endure severe fatigue, lethargy, and a loss of appetite.

Chapter 6

Consternation

Willie rose from the bed, running on little sleep. Although Ivy Lee slept, sleep evaded him for hours. He dreaded having to make the call to Dr. Timmons, but sat down to collect his thoughts before calling. He became more anxious as each finger made the half circle to dial each digit on the black rotary phone, as he sighed.

"Good morning, Dr. Timmons' speaking."

"Good morning, this is Willie Patterson, Ivy Lee's husband."

"Mr. Patterson, how is Mrs. Patterson?"

"Not good, Dr. Timmons. She has been having a lot of spells and does not seem to remember them, and I can't seem to convince her to keep up with her medicine. I don't think she is taking it like she's supposed to."

"Is she violent, or agitated at all?"

"No, she's peaceful, but I have noticed she's pretty down."

"Hmm, the depression appears more pronounced. I would like you to bring her in so I can assess her condition. She needs to be admitted to the hospital. We can observe her and find the best course of treatment and change her medication if needed. Would she be amenable to it?"

"Well, Doc, I don't know, but I will try to encourage her. I know she doesn't like how she's been feeling. I'll talk to her this afternoon and call you in the morning."

"If I'm not available, please call my nurse, and she will arrange for the admission."

"Thank you, Dr. Timmons. Goodbye."

"Goodbye."

Willie felt relieved after speaking with Dr. Timmons. Ivy Lee appeared to be resting. As he sat down to eat another meal alone, he realized how much he missed spending time with Ivy Lee, who was his best friend. He spent the best times in his life with her. It was during these lonely moments he felt the void of not having children of their own. He cherished the time he spent with Riley. *I am going to arrange a fishing trip with him soon*, he thought.

After a few hours, Ivy Lee emerged from the bedroom.

"Hi Baby." She yawned and stretched refreshed entering the living room. "I feel so much better, but I'm hungry."

"Good, I'll heat your food." Willie excited, hurried off to the kitchen.

"Thank you, Willie." She sat down at the dining room table, smoothing the corners of the tablecloth.

Willie laid out the place setting and poured Ivy Lee a tall glass of water in the crystal tumbler. He watched Ivy Lee bless her food and eat and then relayed his conversation with Dr. Timmons presenting the idea of her being admitted to the hospital.

Ivy Lee didn't say a word while he was speaking, but savored every bite of her mashed potatoes, fried chicken, and peas.

"Baby? Did you hear me? What do you think?"

Ivy Lee put her fork down in her now empty plate and peered across the table at Willie.

"Willie, I don't want to go, but I trust you, and I know you wouldn't ask me to go if you didn't think it was best. I'll think about it and let you know tomorrow, Ok?

"Ok baby. I love you, and I need you to get better. You scared me yesterday crossing the street."

"What street, Willie?" She stared at him.

"Don't worry about Ivy Lee. It's ok if you don't remember."

Sonny started fluttering around in his cage and tweeting.

They turned to the cage and smiled.

Ivy Lee sang to Sonny. "Who's the handsomest bird?" Sonny tweeted back, and as usual, Ivy Lee freed him from his cage to fly around the apartment. Willie rose from the couch watching Sonny with his hands on his waist and a wrinkled brow. Sonny flew around the living room, and over to an ecstatic Ivy Lee.

"Ivy Lee, I know you love your bird, but he needs to stay in his cage!" Stunned as he ducked as Sonny soared past his head. He knew Sonny made Ivy Lee happy, but this annoyed him.

"Sonny! go back home," Ivy Lee waved her arm towards Sonny's cage. Sonny retreated to his cage and continued to flutter and tweet. Ivy Lee then turned to Willie displaying a wide grin, and in a gentle tone, "Willie, I'm sorry. I won't do it anymore while you're home, I know you don't like it." She then strode over to Willie giving him a quick peck on the cheek and sauntered into the kitchen.

The afternoon remained quiet. Willie shook off his earlier annoyance with Sonny flying around. They sat close together on the couch and held hands. Willie nodded off while Ivy Lee, with her head on his shoulder, watched their favorite television shows back-to-back through the evening. Ivy Lee secured the lock on Sonny's cage. Once while out of his cage, Sonny perched himself atop Willie's head as he was sleeping. Willie was not happy about it and threatened to open the window and let Sonny fly free. This declaration made Ivy Lee laugh so hard tears formed in her eyes. She knew kindhearted Willie would never release her Sonny. After the kitchen was clean and swept, she kissed him on the forehead to wake him. "Let's go to bed. I'll let you know my decision in the morning. Ok baby?" Willie nodded in agreement.

Ivy Lee's night was restless. Every time she closed her eyes, she pictured the hard bed with the thin blanket from her last hospital stay. Unable to sleep, she lit up a cigarette at the kitchen sink. She held the long cigarette in her right hand while staring at the peach tile above the sink. Feeling the heat on her fingers, she dropped it in the sink.

This broke her gaze, and she headed back to bed. She lay down on the corner of the bed so she wouldn't disturb Willie. Less than an hour into her sleep, she thought she heard a baby cry. She sat up hugging her pillow and rocked back and forth drifting off to sleep.

The next morning, she rose before sunrise scrubbing the floors, while water boiled over on the stove. The table was wet with packages of frozen vegetables and meat defrosting on the table.

"Ivy Lee! Baby, What are you doing? Your pot is boiling over!" He rushed to the stove to turn the burner off, dropping the lid as it burned his finger. He peered into the steamy pot, to see a striped dishcloth floating in the boiling water. Ivy Lee continued humming with a lit cigarette hanging out of her mouth. He shouted her name again, as he went and shook her shoulder. She continued to scrub the floor. "Willie why are you yelling at me. Don't you see me cooking and cleaning? I'm getting tired now, though. Going to lie down."

A stunned Willie watched Ivy Lee as she dropped the scrub brush in the bucket. Her soaking wet nightgown stuck to her body as water dripped down her legs to her bare feet. She tossed her cigarette butt in the sink, kissed Willie on the cheek and exited the kitchen. Willie stood there astounded at the kitchen in disarray, and almost lost his balance on the soapy floor as he reached for the bucket. Confused after witnessing this strange behavior, he scratched his bald head and put the kitchen back in order.

Chapter 7

Ivy Lee's Decision

The next morning Ivy Lee got up confused by her damp nightgown, but she felt rested. She rolled over to see Willie's side empty and realized it was nine o'clock; two hours past Willie's normal start time. As she settled at the kitchen table with her first cup of coffee, she realized she needed to do this for herself, and for Willie. He called to check on her at noon. He was so patient with her over the years and loved her through it. *God made Willie especially for me*, she thought, and she decided she would tell him when he got home.

Even through Ivy Lee's hazy memories and darkest hours, she never lost hope. She had faith she would get clarity and feel normal, even though she didn't know if she would recognize it. She suffered memory lapses after she lost consciousness, waking up in other locations. Those times frightened her, but what terrified her was getting so ill. Willie would tire of her, or Mabel keeping Riley away; *she could never survive it*, she thought.

Willie arrived home at four o'clock sharp. He came straight home unless, there was something to do at the church, which he knew Ivy Lee sometimes resented. He never declined a request from the pastor or from multiple auxiliaries. After he sat down in his favorite chair, he picked up the newspaper. He knew not to pressure Ivy Lee. He didn't want her to shut down, so he would wait for her to let him know her decision.

"Willie I've made my decision. I'll go when you come back from the conference; I know you have been preparing for months.

"Baby don't worry about the conference. I'm concerned about you."

"But I don't want you to miss it. You can have Ida Mae check on me. I promise. I get so scared you won't come back for me." Ivy Lee said as her eyes welled up with tears.

"I would never leave you in there."

"I'm still afraid."

"Ivy Lee, I promise."

Willie sat still as Ivy Lee sat down and grasped his hands while gazing into his eyes. He expected her decision, but stayed silent and took a deep breath.

"I want to do whatever it takes to get better. I will go."

A relieved Willie hugged Ivy Lee. "Okay, then baby. I will let Dr. Timmons know our plan in the morning."

Ivy Lee overheard Willie speaking with Dr. Timmons the next morning, and then Ida Mae on Friday morning. She noticed he was quieter than usual. *He acted this way when he was nervous*, she thought. She tried to allay his fears by reassuring him, she would stick close to home and in close touch with Ida Mae. He promised not to involve Mabel, and Ida Mae promised to call each day Willie was away. They planned a shopping trip downtown. Ivy Lee was calm throughout the week and excited to be getting together with Ida Mae.

Willie woke up before sunrise, surprised to find Ivy Lee cooking him breakfast before he left for Cincinnati. He would pick up Deacon Henry for the three-and-a-half-hour ride. He prayed with Ivy Lee and didn't want to stop hugging her. Even though he knew Ida Mae would check on her, he fidgeted around the house pacing and ask Ivy Lee if she was alright.

Ivy Lee pulled back the beige curtain sheers and peered out the window which overlooked the parking lot. She watched Willie back out and drive away until the car taillights were no longer visible. Her forehead perspired, and her palms became sweaty, as her heart raced, which made her feel dizzy. Frantically pulling at the buttons at the top

33

of her thin pink quilted robe covering her nylon nightgown, she threw it on the couch, and stumbled to sit down. She seemed like she couldn't breathe and grabbed the newspaper from the table to fan herself. Her first inclination was to call Ida Mae, but she didn't want to worry her. She kept fanning herself until she could no longer feel her heart racing and felt calmer. This episode frightened her. She sat still, holding her head, eyes closed until she steadied herself against the wall. *I better get myself together, because I'm in no shape to go the way I'm feeling*, she thought.

Chapter 8

Downtown

Ivy Lee arrived by taxi to Ida Mae's house. They changed into comfortable shoes to go a few blocks over to Twelfth Street to catch the bus downtown to window shop and have lunch at J.L. Hudson's, the major department store.

"Ivy Lee let's sit down for a minute." Ida Mae held Ivy Lee's hand.

"Ivy Lee, you know Willie and all of us care about you. I am here for you." Ida Mae embraced Ivy Lee.

Ivy Lee nodded still upset. "Ida Mae, the hospital scares me, and I don't want to be away from Willie." Ivy Lee shared with Ida Mae about the spell she experienced while in church. She also shared her anxiousness about returning to the hospital for treatment when Willie returns from his trip.

Ivy Lee composed herself, and they headed to the bus stop, a half a block from Ida Mae's house. They took the last vacant seats in the rear of the crowded bus.

They approached the shiny gold elevator to the Mezzanine level at J.L. Hudson's. When the doors opened, they moved to the rear of the crowded elevator. The smell of perfume and cigar tobacco permeated the small space. As the elevator ascended upwards, Ivy Lee felt the flutter in her stomach. She enjoyed elevator rides since she was a child.

The elevator bell chimed upon reaching the Mezzanine level. They made their way from the back of the elevator and headed towards Farmer Street Piccadilly Circus. A huge menu was posted on the wall inside of the entrance, but Ivy Lee already knew what she wanted to order: meatloaf, mashed potatoes, and peas. Her mouth watered as she remembered how this meal tasted homemade. They each picked up a beige plastic tray placing it on the metal counter. Waiting patiently, they collected utensils, and napkins, and made their way down the line. They both splurged on milkshakes in tall crystal soda tumblers; strawberry for Ivy Lee and chocolate for Ida Mae with whipped cream and topped with a cherry. As they found a table in the crowded cafeteria, chatter and the sound of clinking dishes filled the air.

"It was delicious, Ivy Lee. I'm so glad you suggested we come here."

"I enjoyed it too."

They both were full after their meal and left the cafeteria and milled around the greeting card and luggage section. The pair rode the elevator to the second floor to peruse the men's section. Ivy Lee wanted to purchase a new tie for Willie and some monogrammed handkerchiefs. She used the money Willie gave her to buy a new hat. Their last stops were the Budget Store, first and second basements, and the hosiery department.

"Don't let me go in the Millinery department. I don't even want to window shop. Willie needs neckties more than I need hats." They headed out onto Woodward to do more window shopping before heading to the bus stop. The bus wasn't congested, and they could have their choice of vacant seats. Ivy Lee dozed off as soon as she sat down near the back door for the brief ride. Ida Mae leaned over and tapped Ivy Lee on the shoulder to wake her.

"Ivy Lee, we're here." A groggy Ivy Lee leaned forward to see down the center aisle.

She stayed for a half hour chatting with Ida Mae before ordering a taxicab. The ride back home was short, and she struggled to carry her packages up to their third-floor apartment. Thinking to herself she was glad she didn't buy another hat, because she had no more room. Willie hounded Ivy Lee to give away some hats, but she didn't want to part with any of them. She took the tie she bought Willie out of its box holding it up to the light. "I hope he'll like it. Blue is his favorite color."

After she put her stockings and other items away, she sat down on the sofa not realizing how tired she was and fell asleep. She awoke an hour later. It was dusk and the ring from the telephone startled her.

"Hello."

"Hey baby, how are you feeling?"

"Willie! So happy to hear your voice!"

"You sound good. Did you go out with Ida Mae?"

"Yes! We ate at Hudson's and did some window shopping?"

"So pleased to hear it."

"How is the conference?"

"The conference is good. I've met a lot of great people. Even met a Deacon from Jacksonville."

"That's good!"

"Have you taken your medicine?"

"Yes, I have. I'll take a bath and go to bed early. My feet and legs ache."

"You know I'm still worried about you baby, but I'm glad you got out of the house and are feeling better."

"Don't worry. I feel fine baby."

"Ok, but I'll still worry. It's my job. I'll be home on Sunday evening. Get some rest, I'll call you in the morning. Love you."

"I love you too, baby. Goodnight."

As Willie drifted off to sleep, he flashed back to a conference he and Ivy Lee attended together.

Ivy Lee yawned as she and Willie waited by the hotel elevator. They were tired and eager to get to their room from the lengthy four-hour ride to Indianapolis. She got bored with the continuous sight of corn fields on Interstate 24. Willie enjoyed driving and reveled in the country scenery. The rustic majestic barns and the prolific corn fields and bean crops were endless.

"Baby, this reminds me of home. I don't mind driving by the fields, as long as I'm not working them." Willie's high-pitched laugh filling the air. "The best part is we can spend time together." Ivy Lee smiled and reached over and squeezed Willie's warm hand.

The young black elevator operator, dressed in a blue starched shirt, smiled and nodded as they entered. He leaned out, looking both ways to see if anyone else was coming.

"What floor can I take you folks to?" He operated the lever to close the heavy brass elevator doors. The sound of the squeaky brakes squealed as the doors closed.

"Third floor, please."

The operator worked the rickety old elevator with the worn carpet. The car shuddered and shook as it reached their floor. He struggled to line up the floor before it settled.

"Thank you!" Willie waited until Ivy Lee exited first. Ivy Lee returned the smile from the operator.

"You folks have a pleasant stay." He held the door, making sure they were clear of the elevator. Willie nodded and looked down the long hall covered with frayed paisley patterned carpet to search for their room. As they entered the small bathroom, the smell of bleach was present. The smell of tobacco grew stronger as they entered the room. The walls were white, with one worn brown upholstered chair in the corner. Above it was a framed picture of a lighthouse surrounded by choppy water. A big bay window revealed the sundown and a view of the quiet lake. This pleasant memory of Ivy Lee lulled him to sleep.

Chapter 9

Sugar Hill

Ivy Lee took a long hot bubble bath and lay across the bed and fell back asleep wrapped in her bath robe. When she woke up, she turned on the radio. The sound of big band music filled the room. After sitting on the bed awhile and listening to the radio, she went to her closet and searched for her black patent leather strappy sandals not worn in years. Rifling through the closet, she retrieved a dress in an opaque wardrobe bag. She pulled stockings and lingerie from her top drawer. She pinned up her shiny black hair with bobby pins and let the loose curls fall covering one eye. Her eyeliner, blush and lipstick were flawless. She picked up the crystal bottle from the mirrored glass tray containing her favorite perfume, Fleur Sauvage, and pumped the atomizer expressing a light mist. Standing in front of the full-length mirror in their bedroom, pleased with herself, she smiled at her reflection showing the edge of her glimmering gold front tooth. The sound from a car horn outside signaled her of the waiting taxicab. She grabbed her scarf, patent leather purse, and locked the door. She noticed the elderly neighbor across the hall, with her hair in large rollers and a sheer scarf tied at the top, clutching her robe together as she peeked out. Her shocked expression, and a look of disdain washed over Ivy Lee's frame, and she shut her apartment door. Ivy Lee ignored her and made her way down the stairway leading to the apartment's entrance and into the waiting cab.

She stepped out of the taxicab and onto the lit curb. Steadying herself, she sauntered to the door of the Carver Hotel at 87 E. Canfield in the Sugar Hill district.

"Good evening, Ma'am! You're a vision of loveliness tonight." The doorman tipped his hat and opened the door to the club.

The elderly doorman greeted her with a warm smile, while holding the door open. His eyes tracing her plump legs as she took each step towards the door. Inviting sounds of big band jazz seeped out of the open door revealing a packed dance floor in the distance. Couples embraced; hips locked while swaying to the slow melody.

"Thank you." Her eyes adjusted to the dim smokey nightclub as she searched for an empty seat at the crowded bar, and ordered a glass of Jack Daniels. Ivy Lee sipped her drink while bobbing her head. Her legs swayed to the music as she became lost in her thoughts.

"Hey beautiful! I don't believe I've seen you here before." The stranger with a southern drawl appeared through the thick smoke of the jazz nightclub.

Ivy Lee sat silent at the bar with an unlit cigarette hanging from her bright red full lips and appeared oblivious to the stranger's comment.

He was tall, light-skinned, and handsomely dressed in a gray fedora matching his crisp suit. His two-toned wingtip brogue oxfords appeared painted on as he supported one foot on the bottom of the empty bar stool next to Ivy Lee. His cologne drifted up to her nostrils as she closed her eyes to revel in the scent, but not letting on its effect on her. The abrasive friction on the flip top of his silver Zippo lighter made her open her eyes. She felt its warmth, as it illuminated her face. The handsome stranger held the fire to the tip of tobacco protruding from the end of her unfiltered Camel. She took a slow drag and blew the smoke into his face, which didn't deter his interest. The powerful smell of butane hit her nostrils as he closed the top of the lighter.

"Thank you." She eyed him taking in the full view of his muscular frame. Dimples, and the thick mustache framing his straight white teeth. His shiny black wavy hair peeking from under his hat near his ears. She thought back to her Mother's warning about, "dem high yella men" and pivoted her knees away from him.

She pulled at the hem of her dress as she recognized the sound of a Billie Holiday song being played by the band swallowing the remaining whiskey. The attractive stranger was unbothered as she ignored his presence and he continued to gain her attention. She realized the lace of her slip was showing from the side split which exposed her thigh up to her garter belt fastened to her sheer coffee stockings. The red nylon sleeveless dress was low cut, and her large bosom was on full display as the matching scarf fell off one shoulder. The stranger's eyes followed the split down her shapely calf to the ankle strap of her black sandals to the tips of her red painted toes.

"Can I buy you another one of what you are drinking?" he asked as he edged a little closer.

"Sure. Thank you." She turned away bobbing her head to the melody.

"What is your name, beautiful? He pushed the fresh glass of whiskey the bartender refilled closer to her.

"Thanks for the drink, but I won't be here long." Smiled slyly while studying the handsome stranger's physique.

"I want to know your name, beautiful?"

Ivy Lee blushed, but continued to sip her drink, as she heard the host announce the stage was open for amateurs. She gulped the last of her drink and sauntered towards the stage, her hips swaying. The handsome stranger smiled. His eyes followed her as she strutted to the stage. She strolled over to the band leader and whispered to him the song she wanted to sing. Her silk scarf appeared to fall to the base of the microphone stand in slow motion.

The host announced Ivy Lee would be singing, *What a Difference a Day Makes*, by Dinah Washington. Before the first note, Ivy Lee felt nervous; her forehead became shiny with perspiration. She belted out a jazzed-up version of the song, snapping her fingers. The handsome stranger held her gaze to the last note. The club roared with applause. She handed the microphone back to the moderator, picked up her scarf, and headed towards the exit. She asked the doorman to call her

41

a cab and waited near the tall windows by the gold velvet drapes near the entrance. As she waited, the dapper stranger reappeared.

"I enjoyed your performance tonight. It was wonderful!"

"Thank you. By the way, call me Sugar." Batting her long eyelashes as the doorman gestured to her cab's arrival.

Smiling as he rolled the toothpick around between his thin lips. "I'm Blaine." Ivy Lee returned the smile before stepping out of the club and into the waiting cab, waving to the handsome stranger as the cab pulled away.

When the cab descended the freeway ramp, Ivy Lee felt confused and hyperventilated, feeling trapped in the back seat. She tried to calm herself by taking deep breaths. She spotted the driver looking at her through the rearview mirror. When they arrived in front of her apartment, and she paid the fare, she stood confused, looking down at her attire and fumbling through her purse for her keys.

"I'll let you in." shouted a man with his lunchbox exiting the building.

"Thank you!" she said sheepishly and hurried inside.

Chapter 10

Foggy Morning

Ivy Lee could hear the faint sound of the telephone ringing. She threw the covers back and sat up glancing around the room. The bright sun creeping through the curtains hurts her eyes. Her reflection from the mirror shocked her as she moved closer to it. Dressed in a wrinkled red satin dress, stockings; her face smeared with makeup. She froze at her reflection, not remembering putting on this dress and saw her scarf on the floor at the end of the bed. The continuous ring of the phone startled her as she staggered to the front room while grabbing her pounding head.

"Hello." Her voice sounded groggy.

"Ivy Lee! Are you okay? I have been calling you all morning. I didn't want to alarm Willie, so I kept calling."

"Yes, yes, I'm okay, Ida Mae. I slept hard after my bath last night. I'm fine." Ivy Lee replied as she stared down confused by her attire.

"Are you sure? I can come over."

"No, no, I'm fine. I need to eat something. The shopping trip wore me out."

"Me too!"

"Ida Mae, don't worry. I'll call Willie right away. I'm glad you didn't call and upset him. He worries too much."

"I'm so relieved to hear your voice. Get something to eat, and I will call you back this afternoon."

"Bye, Ida Mae. Thanks for checking on me."

Ivy Lee hung up the telephone still stunned by waking up, and not remembering getting dressed. Her purse open on the floor by the door. A book of matches and a tube of lipstick near it. She went over and picked up the unfamiliar matchbook and lipstick. Turning the matchbook over before placing it in her purse, she noticed the name Carver Hotel printed on the cover. Puzzled how it got there, Ivy Lee sat speechless. She tried hard to remember the time between taking her bath last night and awakening in the red dress. Her throbbing head begged for attention. She changed into her duster, wiped the heavy makeup from her flushed face, pushed the dress to the back of her closet, and went to the kitchen to brew some coffee. Sonny fluttered for her attention which took Ivy Lee's mind off her apparent amnesia. Her mind was clear enough to know she couldn't tell Willie or anyone else about it and it upset her she couldn't remember the details of what happened.

As Ivy Lee settled on the sofa, she sat her steaming cup down on the coffee table before her. She held the book of matches in one hand, she reached under the side table for the thick Yellow Pages directory. She flipped through the pages of the enormous book; the breeze of the pages fanned her face as she searched for the hotel category. Her finger rested on the bold printed name of the Carver Hotel. She paused at the telephone number, TY8-1284, and compared it with the number on the matchbook. She closed the directory and shoved it back under the end table. Her hands shook as she fumbled to peel back the cellophane to extract a cigarette from the pack which lay in her lap. She struck a match from the hotel's match book and stared at the flame before putting it to the tip of her cigarette. Inhaling, she blew out the match and dropped it into the heavy green colored glass ashtray on the table.

"I can't remember. This doesn't make sense." She felt calmer with every drag of her cigarette, then napped on the sofa, awaking refreshed and humming a Billie Holiday tune.

Chapter 11

Church Picnic

Ivy Lee looked forward to the annual church picnic. She yawned as she leaned against the kitchen sink. The hot steam from the colander moistened her face. She drained the hot water from the boiled eggs and potatoes for the potato salad she was preparing for the church picnic. The onions and green peppers finely chopped were in a separate bowl. While mixing the ingredients together, she tried to muster up enthusiasm for the day's activities. She loved the annual picnic but felt drained and could feel the dark cloud lurking in the distance. Ivy Lee didn't want to let Willie down, and she got her medicine and a quick bath to calm her nerves. She convinced Willie to postpone her admittance to the hospital by a couple of weeks.

Willie arrived home after leaving the gas station and began transferring the dishes Ivy Lee prepared to their car. Ivy Lee felt much better after her brief nap and bath, and slipped into a simple plaid skirt and white blouse. She couldn't wait to spend time with Ida Mae and other church members.

Many event and church picnic signs cluttered each side of the entrance to the busy park. The church reserved the largest shed. As Willie pulled up next to the shed to unload, the perfect view of the Detroit River emerged. The water was a greenish-blue, and the scene calmed her. She hoped they would have a little time later to stroll along the river's edge. Children ran to the car eager to see her as she exited the car. A little girl with two long thick shiny braids, and wearing pink checkered shorts and a pink and white top, ran throwing her arms around Ivy Lee's waist.

"We missed you Mrs. Patterson! Come sit at our table." She chattered.

This gentle gesture touched Ivy Lee as she made her way to the picnic table. She felt comfortable and realized how much she missed feeling somewhat normal with her church family. Willie headed over, but stopped before reaching the table as he observed Ivy Lee engrossed in talking to the other ladies about their favorite soap operas and new recipes. He returned to set up games for the children and marveled at how happy Ivy Lee seemed. Everything seemed perfect in this moment. There was a warm breeze blowing off the river. He whispered to Ivy Lee he didn't forget their planned stroll.

The vast park was bustling with visitors. Individual picnics surrounded the grassy area, with blankets, picnic tables, and the smell of burning charcoal. Ivy Lee excused herself from the group of ladies to take a short stroll to the restroom in the distance. She exited the restroom and noticed a man leaned over the water fountain. She removed her sunglasses and stopped to wipe her sweaty forehead before making her way back to the shed.

"Sugar! Sugar!" The man called as he raised up from the porcelain fountain, water dripping from his thick black mustache.

Ivy Lee turned surveying the surrounding area. *He couldn't be talking to me*, she thought.

"I'm Blaine. You told me your name was, Sugar, right?" He paused. "Did I get it wrong? We met at the Carver Hotel."

Ivy Lee's eyes widened. Beads of perspiration appeared across her forehead, but she kept strolling and quickened her pace. She didn't recognize this man and thought he must be mistaken. She continued towards the shed, but the man ran up beside her.

"I saw you over there." He tilted his head towards the shed. "Church picnic? I don't want to bother you, Sugar. Just wanted to say hello. How nice it was meeting you at the Carver. Your voice is beautiful." Ivy Lee stopped and took off her sunglasses glaring the strange man in his eyes.

"You must have mistaken me. The Carver?"

"It's ok, Sugar, I get it, church picnic by day, nightclub at night. I hope to see you there again. Have a great day beautiful." He winked and headed over to a crowded picnic table.

Ivy Lee returned to the table. All four of the women at the table were staring at her. Each of them wearing various colored patterned or floral sleeveless summer dresses and sandals or tennis shoes. Mother Anderson, the first to query Ivy Lee, was the oldest member at the table, sported a big straw hat with two thick long gray braids peeking out. Her large arms planted on the arms of the green and white folding webbed lawn chair positioned at the end of the picnic table. Her obese frame protruded from each side of the chair and her metal walker posted close by.

"Baby, who were you chatting with?" Mother Anderson leaned forward.

Ivy Lee, with no expression. "Oh, Mother Anderson, he was a man who thought I was someone else."

Ivy Lee ended the conversation and picked up a paper plate from the table. "Mother Anderson did you have some of my sweet potato pie, I made it just for you!" She headed to the opposite end of the long table to a covered container labeled peach cobbler.

Lifting the aluminum foil, she shrieked, "Mother Anderson is this your peach cobbler!" quickly changing the subject. She saw Mother Anderson lean back in her chair with a questioning expression on her face.

The whole encounter was strange to her, but she stayed focused on enjoying the company of her church family and later Willie took her across the road to the river. Once at home, she recalled finding the matchbook a few weeks ago with Carver Hotel printed on it. The thought made her anxious because it was all she could remember; it was unnerving the stranger in the park also mentioned it. She couldn't remember, but felt it was something Willie shouldn't know.

Depression returned following the church picnic. Ivy Lee moped around the house. Dark circles enveloped her eyes, and she hadn't bathed in days. She tossed and turned all night, muttering and flailing her arms.

"Baby, don't you think it's time to see Dr. Timmons." Ivy Lee stared as tears rolled down her cheeks. Nodding her head, she turned and retreated to the bedroom.

Chapter 12

Northlawn

After an hour, the sound of the receptionist's squeaky footsteps returned closer to the lounge.

"Nurse Emily will be right out to check Mrs. Patterson in."

"Ok. Thank you." Willie wrung his hands.

More waiting Willie thought. He didn't want Ivy Lee to go, but he knew she needed help. As he pulled her closer to him, the lump forming in his throat grew more intense. The pressure of Ivy Lee's moist forehead against his cheek, caused him to reminisce back to the time they began courting. *The most stunning woman he laid eyes on*, he thought. Her innocent child-like quality exuded a bit of mystery. The first time he saw her, he was visiting her home church, St. James Baptist Church.

The small church was packed with parishioners on a stifling humid Easter Sunday. He recalled Ivy Lee's light-yellow dress, matching hat, and white gloves. The material hung on her ample curves. His eyes followed her shapely legs down to her white patent leather shoes. She mesmerized him. After the first offering, Ivy Lee led the most beautiful version of *Blessed Assurance*, he'd ever heard. He later learned it was her favorite hymn, followed by *We'll Understand it Better By and By*. Her eyes caught his gaze as she took her seat in the choir stand. Her beautiful, coifed hair hung in loose curls to frame her heart-shaped face. Long dark eyelashes highlighted her dark brown almond-shaped eyes set above her high cheekbones. Her full lips painted in bright red lipstick complimented her copper complexion.

49

"Mr. and Mrs. Patterson?" Nurse Emily's voice startled Willie.

"Yes," Willie stood, while lifting Ivy Lee's hand to prompt her to rise from the couch.

"Come right this way."

With much trepidation, they followed the slender nurse down the sparsely lit corridor. Her stiff nurse's cap perched against her tight auburn bun. Ivy Lee's steps were more like a slow shuffle. They stopped at the only room lit in the dark quiet corridor.

"Mr. Patterson, this is where your wife will be staying." Nurse Emily said as she unlocked the heavy steel door. The stale cold air enveloped them as they both stood there staring at each other.

"May I call you, Ivy Lee?"

Ivy Lee nodded, never raising her head to make eye contact with Nurse Emily.

"Come on, Sweetie." She ushered Ivy Lee towards the bed in the far edge of the room. Ivy Lee sat down on the rigid mattress topped with a white sheet covered by a thin green blanket. She surveyed the room, tears welling up in her eyes. A small green metal nightstand was in an opposite corner and a narrow brown metal door which led to a tiny bathroom held a small porcelain basin and a toilet.

"Mr. Patterson, we recommend you wait at least a week before visiting. We want to keep your wife focused on her treatment and get her acclimated to her surroundings without distractions. Here is a number you can call to check on her. Do you have questions?" Nurse Emily handed the white card out to Willie.

"No Ma'am," Willie squeezed Ivy Lee's sweaty palm and took the card from Nurse Emily.

"Sweetie, I have to leave you now, but I will check on you. You will be fine. I'm so glad you are taking this step." An exhausted Willie hugged Ivy Lee as he stroked her back. Her warm tears wet the shoulder of his plaid shirt. He kissed her on her lips plodding towards the door stopping to glance back at his Ivy Lee before turning the doorknob to exit.

"I love you, Sweetie."

"I love you, Willie." Ivy Lee hoarsely whispered.

As Willie entered the hall, he noticed muted pale green walls, and the burned-out fluorescent lights lining the ceiling. It was quiet for a massive building which was filled with staff and patients. Willie took the slow stride to the car and sat for a few minutes. His fingers on the key, but not turning it to start the ignition. It was rare for them to spend time apart. He dreaded going back to their empty apartment alone.

On the forty-five-minute drive back to Detroit, Willie prayed the treatment would help to relieve some of the anguish she went through. Ivy Lee's mood swings could change from being filled with so much energy, cheerful, singing and cleaning the entire house, to dark times when she couldn't get out of bed. Crying spells and immense confusion could last for days. The most confusing times were her describing hearing voices or seeing things not there. During her confusion, she couldn't find her way to the bedroom. She kept going in the kitchen searching for the bedroom door.

As Willie settled in, he noticed a crumbled piece of paper on Ivy Lee's side of the bed. It portrayed a sketch of a baby with the name Georgia scratched out. He thought little of it because he knew Ivy Lee loved to draw and color. The vivid pictures in her coloring books were picturesque. She blended the crayon colors and then used a tissue to mix and smooth them into a whole new color. Riley, who loved to spend time with her, often wanted her to draw or color a picture for him when they were together.

The cold empty bed felt so huge with Ivy Lee away. He placed the paper on their nightstand and then curled up near her side cradling her pillow. Inhaling her favorite perfume, English Lavender, he drifted off to sleep. He tried to rest, but kept waking up every hour to glance at the clock.

The next morning as he put on his coffee, he tried to relax at the kitchen table. He pulled the black telephone with the long cord into the kitchen and dialed the hospital. The phone seemed to ring forever.

"Good morning, Northlawn Hospital." The cheery receptionist answered.

"This is Willie Patterson. I'm calling to check on my wife, Ivy Lee."

"Good morning, Mr. Patterson. I am Nurse Tracie. I came on duty after you left. Nurse Emily said your wife became upset after you left, and we sedated her with pethidine. She was still asleep when I checked on her on my last round. Please call back in a couple of hours."

"Thank you, Goodbye."

Bewildered, Willie fumbled to put the telephone back on the receiver. He didn't have an appetite, but sat at the table sipping his cold coffee. He knew Ivy Lee would want him to eat and he tried, but couldn't muster up an appetite. Tired from his restless night without Ivy Lee, he lay down for an hour. Pulling up the blanket he discovered a matchbook cover with the name of the Carver Hotel on it in her open nightstand drawer. Finding it odd and inspecting it for a moment, he tossed it back in the drawer. Tiredness took over, and he lay back on the pillow and fell asleep.

Chapter 13

Mabel and Randall

Mabel received the news from Willie about Ivy Lee's admission to the hospital. She hoped she was getting the help she needed. She tried to remain optimistic, but sometimes Ivy Lee's progress didn't last. After she hung up, she remembered the appointment she scheduled with a prospective tenant to tour the vacant upstairs flat and rushed upstairs to make sure everything was ready. She evicted the last tenant who moved in after Willie and Ivy Lee because of non-payment of rent. Mabel didn't play about her money.

***

Her home was immaculate and quiet except on the occasion Randall drank too much.

"Mabel! Mabel!" He would call out staggering in the side door, keys jingling, his fingers feeling for the light switch in the hallway. His heavy footsteps leading to the upstairs flat would wake Mabel. "Baby, you know I love you!" he slurred. *He's confused again,* she thought. She heard him making his way up the back stairs to the upstairs flat. His feet clumping on each step. This was a common pattern with Randall. Mabel would coax him back down the stairs, his arm around her shoulder and his weight shifting back and forth. They both staggered as she tried to keep him upright to guide him into their lower flat. She worried this would annoy her tenants.

"Randall, baby you have got to stop! You drink too much!" Randall ignored her and belted out a song and proclaimed his love for Mabel. His speech garbled."I love you baby."

He wakened the morning after these binges, head pounding, not remembering the night before. Judging by Mabel's demeanor and response to him, he knew it couldn't be good. She initially gave him a hard time. He usually came home with flowers and a profound remorseful apology. Randall was a good man. He adopted Riley without hesitation giving him his last name.

Randall and Riley were the only ones who brought out Mabel's softer side. She was an excellent Mother, although overprotective.

Mabel struggled to get Randall settled in bed with his tall husky frame which towered over her at six and a half feet. He passed out before he fell face down on the bed. His filthy work boots caked with mud still on as Mabel wrangled them off each foot. She never allowed him to wear his coveralls and work boots in the house. If sober, he would remove them at the side door. He didn't flinch, but continued to snore loudly with his mouth wide open.

Mabel stood back and admired this man even in this miserable state. They were opposites, who found each other, and her love for him never wavered. He was a good provider and although they worshiped different religions, she knew he was a spiritual man who loved God. Randall worshipped at the Methodist church, and Mabel a devout Jehovah's Witness. He faithfully read his Bible every night before going to bed.

Randall woke up to the smell of hickory bacon. His head thumped as he rolled over to swing his feet around and into a wobbly stance, while putting his hand to his forehead. He stumbled to the bathroom to throw water on his face and relieve his swelling bladder. He couldn't remember the previous night, but he hoped Mabel was not mad at him. After he sweet-talked his way back in, his plan was to take Riley fishing. She knew he would never drink around Riley, although he, occasionally consumed a few drinks too many after his Friday card game with the guys at the shop; They debated sports and politics more than playing cards.

"Randall! Come to breakfast!" Still upset from his antics, but she knew he was hungover.

"Ok, I'm coming!" His head still throbbing.

He took it as a good sign. *She didn't sound mad*, he thought. As he entered the kitchen, the aroma of fresh coffee reached his nostrils.

"Sit on down, baby. Everything is ready."

"Thank you, baby." he responded cautious but relieved, took his seat, as his mouth watered.

"I was thinking about taking Riley fishing, and maybe Little Charles can join us. Do you have any plans for him today?"

"No, sounds good. He will be excited."

Riley and Little Charles chattered for the entire ride to Belle Isle. He couldn't wait to get to the Detroit River's edge. Mabel packed sandwiches and a plastic jug of fresh squeezed lemonade. She also packed a few of Riley's favorite homemade peanut butter cookies with the crisscross pattern on top. She hid them way down at the bottom of the picnic basket in the hopes they wouldn't eat them first.

Willie declined their invitation. The trio returned with a cooler full of pickerel for Mabel to clean. She didn't eat fish, but she cleaned and fried it until it was a crispy golden brown. *Now I don't have to figure out today's dinner*, she thought.

Chapter 14

Ivy Lee's Diagnosis

The house was eerily silent without Ivy Lee. The few days were hard on Willie. He refused to sleep in their bed without her. He sat up in the overstuffed chair until he dozed off. The next morning, his coworkers noticed how quiet he was all week. They missed his contagious high-pitched laughter. Willie shrugged and said he was fine and tried to get through the week.

When he called, Dr. Timmons reported she was having a difficult time adapting and asked he not visit until the weekend. He complied but couldn't help but worry. Having no appetite, he tried to eat. *Ivy Lee would want me to.* He thought.

Willie had a thin build and an immense appetite, but he never picked up weight. The guys at the sanitation yard would tease him about his slight frame while observing him lifting heavy garbage cans all day.

Ivy Lee felt foggy, as she heard a knock on the door. It was Dr. Timmons. His rubber soles stuck to the waxy floor with every step he took towards her.

"Mrs. Patterson, it's Dr. Timmons. How do you feel this morning?"

"I don't feel myself. I feel shaky. Can I tell you about something else I have been feeling before my Willie gets here?"

"Yes, please. That's what I'm here for."

Ivy Lee described the strange man who approached her at the church picnic who seemed to recognize her and told her they met at a club. She didn't recognize him, nor did she have any memory of attending a club. Later she found a book of matches in a purse with the club's name written on it. The memory of waking up in the red apparel flooded back. She said it was confusing, and she couldn't remember the details at all, but her interaction with the stranger felt vaguely familiar.

"He also said I've sung at the nightclub and told him my name was Sugar." Her eyes watered and she covered her face with her hands. "I'm so confused Dr. Timmons. What is happening to me?"

"Well, Mrs. Patterson, I suspected there were other conditions you may have been experiencing from some things you revealed in our therapy sessions, but this seems to confirm it. The memory lapses are consistent with what we call Dissociative amnesia or Dissociate fugue. These big words only mean you have a memory loss. This includes time you can't account for, and unfamiliar places or situations which you find yourself in; things out of your character. This is a lot to take in. Do you understand?"

"No, I don't understand. I know there are a lot of things I don't remember. Please don't tell Willie what I have told you."

"Mrs. Patterson, I will respect your wishes. You are my patient and I want you to feel comfortable sharing your feelings. What we discuss is confidential unless you tell me otherwise. We will continue to work through this during our therapy sessions. The medicine the nurse gave you should help you calm down. I will see you tomorrow." He headed towards the door. Ivy Lee sat there still stunned but feeling the effects of the medicine taking effect.

Filled with worry, but eager to see Ivy Lee, Saturday morning arrived, and Willie headed to Northlawn to arrive at noon, the start of visiting hours. The thin gray-haired nurse led him to Ivy Lee's room. Ivy Lee sat on the edge of the bed. She appeared disheveled in her wrinkled gown, wearing one sock and her hair in disarray.

"Ivy Lee, baby, I'm here!" He rushed to her side.

"Willie?" Willie sat down on the bed next to Ivy Lee. She put her head on his shoulder and let out an enormous sigh.

"I thought you were never coming back, Willie. You left me here and I'm scared."

Willie noticed Ivy Lee's words slurred. He lifted her chin to view her eyes which wouldn't focus.

"I would never leave you and not come back, baby. How are you feeling?"

"I feel confused Willie and I keep having dreams about when I was young, and dreams of a baby, and hearing the name Georgia. The same dream over and over. Willie there are also times when I lose track of time and can't remember. It scares me."

"Did you tell Dr. Timmons about it?"

"Yes, I think I did. Sometimes I'm sleepy when he visits. I try to stay awake, but I can't."

Willie held Ivy Lee the rest of the visit holding her, caressing her back, face, and hair, while planting kisses on her temple. He retrieved her missing sock from between the sheets and blanket, and straightened her gown fastening it correctly. Finally convincing her to lie down, he continued to massage her back until she wandered off to sleep. A lump formed in his throat as he witnessed Ivy Lee in this vulnerable state. He covered her up with the thin worn green blanket and backed away to the door being careful not to wake her. The same nurse was waiting outside of Ivy Lee's room.

"Is Dr. Timmons available?"

"Yes, I think he is. Please wait for him in the lounge."

"Thank you."

Willie made his way to the drab lounge and took a seat in the corner, holding his brown hat by the rim. Although the sun glowed through the dusty blinds, the room felt dim to him, as he peered at the dull tile floor.

"Mr. Patterson? How are you?"

Willie noticed Dr. Timmons in his starched white lab coat. His dark rimmed reading glasses perched at the end of his nose, and his wispy gray hair coifed at the hairline. Willie rose to shake his hand as they both took a seat on the worn leather sofa.

"Thank you for waiting until now to visit. We are still adjusting her medication. She is a little drowsy. I assure you; it is normal as we get to the right level for her. She has been experiencing other symptoms related to a type of amnesia. We will continue therapy while she is here and continue with this treatment plan after she goes home."

"Yes, I noticed, and I'm concerned. I'm relieved though she's not agitated. When can I take her home?"

"We need to see how the medicine affects her as we decrease the dosage. She received two medications which work together. We need to monitor her closely. I will know more in a week. We want to control her anxiety, and we noticed she is also experiencing a bit of amnesia and schizophrenia. Has she mentioned seeing or hearing things?

"No." Willie dumbfounded.

"Patients who exhibit schizophrenia, express hearing voices and seeing things which aren't there. We want the best treatment plan for her, one she can maintain. Too often patients stop taking the meds before they have given it enough time to metabolize or level off in their system. We want to ensure she functions as normal as possible. Do you understand, Mr. Patterson?"

"Ok, I think I understand it better now. She keeps bringing up dreams of a baby. She wakes up sometimes holding the pillow as if she is rocking a baby. Has she mentioned it to you, Dr. Timmons?"

"No not specifically. Do you have any more questions?"

"No, I feel a little better now you've explained it. Thank you."

"Mr. Patterson, thank you for your patience with the process. She needs your support."

Dr. Timmons stood up and patted Willie on the back with one hand while giving him a firm handshake.

"See you soon."

Chapter 15

Mabel Visits Northlawn

Mabel peered through the crisscross of the safety glass to Ivy Lee's sanatorium room. The heavy hospital doors, which lined the long corridor of the hospital wing, muffled moans, screams, and murmurs. She could see Ivy Lee sitting, legs crossed on the end of the bed rocking. Mabel impatiently tapping her foot as the stern orderly dressed all in white unlocked the door to Ivy Lee's room.

"Mrs. Patterson, you have a visitor." Ivy Lee raised her head slowly. Her hair was in disarray and the snaps on her hospital gown fastened out of sequence caused it to bunch up. The nurse waited outside.

"Sister?"

"Yes, Ivy Lee, I'm here, how are you?"

"I don't know, I'm confused, where am I?"

"You are in a place where they can help you. Willie brought you here."

"I'm scared, Sister, they tied me up." Mabel noticed the unfastened leather restraints on the bed rails.

"Ivy Lee, they didn't want you to hurt yourself."

"Can I ask you something, Sister?"

"Yes, Ivy Lee, anything." Mabel scanned the sparse room.

"I have been having this dream. It's about a baby. Something bad happened to her, but I can't remember."

"Ivy Lee, I don't want to upset you, we can chat about your dream later. You have been on a lot of medicine to help you. It's most likely the cause of those dreams."

"Why won't you tell me, Mabel? I'm not crazy, it can't be a dream!"

As Ivy Lee hung her head, Mabel noticed her trembling, and the top of her green wrinkled hospital gown showed droplets.

"Calm down Ivy Lee, you have upset yourself."

Ivy Lee paced across the shiny tile floor. Her bare feet shuffled towards the window and then back to the bed. Ivy Lee stopped pacing abruptly and turned around and stopped directly in front of Mabel. Her demeanor was calm, and her hands suddenly became steady.

"Her name was Georgia!" she screamed in a low raspy tone.

Mabel stunned, moved towards Ivy Lee to embrace her. Ivy Lee backed away and faced the window and repeated, "Georgia, Georgia, Baby Georgia." as tears streamed down her face. Mabel's eyes widened, and she stood frozen.

Ivy Lee finally felt calm. A repeated rotation of memories washed over her. She didn't want to believe it was real. Her recollection of the tragedy which took place back in Wadesboro became clear. It started with Mabel in charge while both of their parents were at work; Tommie down the road taking care of the Green family's children and other household tasks, and their father Johnny, a sharecropper, was out in the fields. It was a scorching afternoon. Ivy Lee cuddled on the old sofa and begged to rock Georgia to sleep.

"I remember!" Ivy Lee screamed. Mabel swiftly exited. The nurse appearing further down the corridor. Once in the hallway she rested against the wall closing her eyes and exhaling deeply "Oh my God, she remembers."

***

The next morning, Ivy Lee's cloudy memory seemed clearer than she experienced for some time. She knew by the expression on Mabel's face Georgia was real. She also knew she was dead, but the circumstances were unclear. Ivy Lee remembered rocking her to sleep and waking to the wails and screams of Tommie and Mabel. She woke up in the cold soggy fields covered in mud. She didn't know how she got home. She remembered Mabel suffered bouts of crying for weeks and wouldn't come near her.

Chapter 16

Baby Georgia

Baby Georgia was a tiny little thing, born one month premature; barely weighed eight pounds at two- and one-half months old. She was light-skinned with thick curly hair and enormous hazel eyes.

Ivy Lee was the only one who could keep her quiet, so Mabel gave in. Ivy Lee changed Baby Georgia's diaper, and gently swaddled her in the pink blanket Tommie knitted for her. She lay on her lap while rocking her to sleep, singing a sweet lullaby in her beautiful soprano voice. Once she was completely asleep, Ivy Lee put Georgia on her side near the inside of the couch as she stretched down on the edge, protecting her baby sister.

Soon the clear skies turned dark, and the curtains vigorously blew, but with it came a pleasant cool breeze, which lulled Ivy Lee to sleep. She was a restless sleeper, but a violent thunderstorm was soothing to her.

Around dusk, Tommie returned from her long day, entering the small, sparsely furnished living room. Frank was eager for the rain to cease, so he could go outside. Mabel sat in the big rocking chair, resting after she cooked a big pot of butter beans. Tommie with one hand on her hip. "Did you get all of your chores done?"

"Yes, Mama, and Ivy Lee rocked Georgia to sleep while I was cooking. She seems to be the only one who can calm her."

Tommie turned around to see Ivy Lee, hanging halfway off the couch with stuffing coming out of every cushion seam, but she didn't see Georgia. Tommie glanced towards the back bedroom. "Where is Georgia? Did she put her in her crib in the bedroom?"

"No Mama, she is lying right beside Ivy Lee." Mabel marched back into the kitchen.

Tommie went to where they lay and let out a gut-wrenching scream. When Ivy Lee shifted, Tommie could see Georgia wedged between the bottom cushion and the cushion back of the sofa. Tommie quickly grabbed Georgia and rolled her over. Her tiny, sweet face was pale, and her lips had turned blue.

"What did you do? What did you do? Tommie screamed at a sleeping Ivy Lee.

Ivy Lee groggily sat up, still half-asleep, wondering if she was dreaming. Ivy Lee's eyes widened as she saw Tommie holding a limp, lifeless Georgia. She moved closer in disbelief. When she realized Baby Georgia was dead, she began sobbing so heavily she couldn't catch her breath. Mabel screaming, she killed Georgia until Ivy Lee wrangled herself away as Mabel fell to her knees, wailing loudly.

"I rocked her to sleep, Mama. I didn't do nothing. My baby! My baby!" she screamed as she ran out the door into the muddy yard, heading towards the dense fields.

Chapter 17

Anguish

The events of that day forever changed Ivy Lee. Her mind was foggy and confused. She only remembered lying down and being violently shaken by Mabel, who was screaming as their Mother shouted.

Ivy Lee's father found her hiding in the fields in the pouring rain. She repeated this memory each time she found herself caught in the rain; She never understood the connection, only knew the rain caused her anxiety, followed by an icy chill around her ankles.

Her clothes stuck to her body, drenched by the rain and caked in mud. Her father put his arm around her while he guided her back to the house in the chilly rain. She stopped crying as her teeth chattered. She seemed like she was moving in slow motion. Her father said he called out to her for some time. She couldn't move or speak and appeared to be in a daze. It felt like a dream. Tommie embraced her as she wrapped a towel around her and led her towards the fireplace. She glanced at the corner where Georgia's bassinet used to be, but it was bare. Frank, sitting in the corner facing away from Ivy Lee, got up to give her a brief hug. It was then she saw his red eyes. He returned to his chair and fidgeted with a ragged baseball. "It's not your fault, Ivy Lee. It was an accident." She sobbed again as Tommie cradled her head in her lap. The house was still ever since Georgia died.

***

They held the burial at the modest family cemetery near the end of their small field. Mabel took it hard. She hardly spoke to Ivy Lee since the day of Georgia's death. The tiny wooden box was so small. Ivy Lee, Mabel, and Frank followed their parents. Several neighbors, their pastor, and his wife gathered around the shallow grave, while Pastor Williams said a few words, committing the tiny casket to the ground.

As they headed away from the graveyard, Ivy Lee saw Frank's friend, Ozias Johnson, with his parents, heading back towards the road. His Mother embraced Tommie and took a flowered handkerchief out of her purse and handed it to crying Mabel. Mabel took it and dabbed her tear-stained cheeks, as she began a slow pace towards the house. Ivy Lee was the last one standing over the small mound of dark soil where Georgia lay. Frank, Ivy Lee's protector, turned and grabbed her hand and led her back to the house.

Chapter 18

Change of Scenery

The start of summer constantly reminded Ivy Lee of the summer she spent in Raleigh. It was the summer of 1962, and she was so excited to visit her Aunt Dena and Uncle David in Raleigh. She was a small girl the last time she saw them. Tommie sent her to help her Aunt Dena who was recuperating from a broken leg and needed help with cooking and cleaning. Ivy Lee never gave Tommie any trouble and regularly helped around the house. It would be her first time riding the bus to Raleigh alone. Her older cousin Van would pick her up from the bus station. Van, their only child, was a few years older than Ivy Lee.

Ivy Lee slept most of the two-hour ride. She hadn't seen Van since they were kids, and she was not sure she would recognize him, but he was the only person who appeared to be waiting for someone.

Ivy Lee was seventeen but appeared much older. Van barely got a word in between Ivy Lee's banter about how excited she was to visit. Van opened the car door for her and loaded her one suitcase in the back seat. She planned to stay a month, which would give her a break from Mabel. She hoped she could persuade Aunt Dena into piercing her ears. Tommie insisted she wait until she was eighteen, and she felt she'd waited long enough.

They pulled up to the old frame house with the big porch. Uncle David perched on the porch swing. His cheek bulging with snuff, and he held a spittoon in his left hand.

He rose to greet Ivy Lee while setting down his snuff can.

"Ivy Lee! I'm so glad to see you! You're all grown up now. Your Aunt Dena is waiting for you." He said as he hugged Ivy Lee. His wiry beard scratching her cheek as she got a whiff of the stale tobacco snuff on his breath.

"Van show Ivy Lee in there. Your Mama is waiting on her."

"It's good to see you Uncle David." She followed Van who held the front door open.

Her eyes adjusted to the light in the dark stuffy house. There were family pictures on every wall. Trinkets covered every table. She turned her head to see the large dining room table which held a dusty punch bowl.

"Ivy Lee! Come on in here!" Aunt Dena squealed. Ivy Lee entered the bedroom beyond the dining room to see Auntie Dena braced up in the huge oak bed with large bed posts. Ivy Lee ran over to Aunt Dena but stopped to maneuver around her leg which was in a cast propped up on a large pillow. Van stood and watched the two in a long embrace. Aunt Dena, tears in her eyes, wiped them with her wrinkled handkerchief.

"I'm so happy to see you Aunt Dena!" beamed Ivy Lee.

"I've missed you chile. You've grown up on me. Pull a chair up. We need to catch up."

"Yes, we do Auntie. I have missed you, and I love it here in Raleigh."

"Van you're free to go. I know you want to see your friends."

Grinning at the two of them, Van kissed his Mother on the cheek. "Yes Ma'am. I'll see you two later."

"Bye Ivy Lee."

"Bye."

They chatted for hours, and Ivy Lee asked Aunt Dena to pierce her ears. After breakfast the next morning, she got her wish. Aunt Dena set up everything for the piercing.

"Morning! Ivy Lee. Baby come on over here. Let's get those ears done. Pull a chair over here. I've got everything set up." Ivy Lee was excited until she spotted the sewing needle on the table. Her eyes widened, as she nervously sat down, but she knew she couldn't back out. Aunt Dena sterilized the needle from the stove's flame. She quickly numbed her ear with ice and placed a piece of raw potato behind it. Before Ivy Lee could squeal at the pain, it was over. Aunt Dena told her to keep the ice on it to ease the pain and followed with some witch hazel.

"Chile you did good. You didn't flinch. Get me the broom in the corner." Ivy Lee thought the request was strange but followed directions. Aunt Dena pulled out one bristle from the top of the broom, broke it in a small piece, burned it on both ends from the stove's flame. "Ok come on over here." She placed the straw in the first ear and repeated the process for the second ear. Ivy Lee barely noticed the pain from the second ear because the first ear was still throbbing, but glad it was over. She hoped her Mother wouldn't be upset with Aunt Dena.

"Those ears have to heal. Don't be touching em and keep putting this witch hazel on em ya hear. You don't want them to get infected." Ivy Lee relieved, thanked her.

Ivy Lee enjoyed her time in Raleigh. She spent her days cooking and assisting Aunt Dena and spending some evenings with Van and a few of his friends, who seemed to hang around the house as if they lived there. One of Van's friend, Gary, seemed to be attracted to her. He liked to sing and seemed to sing directly to her. Singing was one thing they shared. He was in his church's choir and convinced the choir director to let Ivy Lee sing with them. He asked if he could take her to the movies. She told him she would need permission from Aunt Dena.

The two were inseparable throughout the summer. She knew she would return to Wadesboro soon. She already stayed a month longer than planned. Gary, a college student at Fayetteville State, six feet tall, thin, and a sharp dresser was a gentleman. She never met boys like him back in Wadesboro; the boys back home were immature, would leer, especially Ozias. She couldn't understand what Mabel could have seen in him.

Gary wanted to be a teacher and wanted Ivy Lee to visit the campus. Ivy Lee never thought about college, nor did she imagine life beyond her little country town. She didn't let Aunt Dena know she cried the night she said goodbye to Gary. They vowed to write, and he said he would visit on his break, but it never transpired.

Ivy Lee's return home was only a few weeks away. She liked Raleigh and the time she spent with Aunt Dena. Aunt Dena could use a cane after her cast was off. They enjoyed long conversations when Ivy Lee would braid her hair. She felt comfortable sharing how she would sometimes get sad about Georgia and how much she missed Frank. She didn't feel like she could discuss it with Tommie or Mabel. Thinking about the way Frank cared for her made her emotional.

Aunt Dena was so excited to be going to a movie with Uncle David. Her gait was not perfectly steady yet, but she dressed up in her favorite sleeveless powder blue cotton shift dress. Uncle David smiled as he opened the creaky car door for her.

***

Ivy Lee sat alone and barefoot at the old, faded wood piano in the corner, and dabbed the ivory keys and wished she knew how to play a tune. After Van left, the house was quiet.

"Hey there! Anyone home?" Ivy Lee crept towards the screen door and recognized, Uncle David's nephew Samuel who she found attractive. He was of average height, smooth dark skin, clean shaven, a sharp dresser with a gap tooth grin like Uncle David. He was handsome, and he knew it, and continuously tried to impress Van by bragging of all his exploits with women. She heard Aunt Dena say he was no good; he had a wife and children and fathered children all over Raleigh. Even this didn't stop Ivy Lee from secretly being enamored with him.

"Hey Samuel. Auntie and Uncle are out right now. I will tell them you came by." She announced as she leaned provocatively against the inside of the door frame. Her head slightly tilted and twirling her hair around her finger.

"Ok. When will they be back? My car is making a noise and Uncle David said he would check it out."

"I'm not sure, they went to see a movie."

"Hey gal, it's hot out here, does Auntie have any sweet tea?" Samuel took off his hat and fanned himself.

"I think so. I'll check." Ivy Lee went into the kitchen and poured Samuel a mason jar full of sweet tea and added a fresh slice of lemon and returned to the door.

"Here you go, Samuel." Ivy Lee opened the screen door with enough space to hand him the glass.

"Thanks, gal." He anxiously grabbed the glass slightly touching her hand.

"You're welcome." She bashfully backed away.

"Come sit out here with me. I don't bite." He patted the space on the porch swing next to him.

A barefoot Ivy Lee hesitantly came out on the porch. She sat on the opposite end of the swing.

"This tea is good! You know what would make it better?" He pulled a small flask from his inside pocket, quickly twisting off the top and pouring the brown liquid into his cup of tea and taking a big gulp. Ivy Lee watched curiously.

"A little spice. Want to taste it? I won't tell, gal." He offered the glass to Ivy Lee, who declined at first, but sheepishly accepted and took a tiny sip.

"So, what do you think? It's good, ain't it? A little ain't gonna hurt you. Go ahead, have some more."

Ivy Lee drank half of the glass and handed it back to Samuel seeing the devious grin on his face.

"You kind of liked it, huh?" Samuel snickered. "It's ok, I won't tell nobody. Especially your Auntie. It will be our secret." He chuckled. They chatted awhile longer. With him leading the conversation and bragging about himself. The whole time, Samuel complimented Ivy Lee's appearance. His jokes made her laugh and before long, she felt comfortable and began flirting with him. She had never received such attention from a grown man. In comparison, Gary was a boy, Samuel was at least 30 years old, and his interest flattered her even though she knew it shouldn't, but it intrigued her.

Ivy Lee smiled. "I have to finish the dishes before they get back. I'll tell Uncle David you came by. You can leave the glass on the banister. I'll get it later."

"Ok, gal", he said as his eyes followed her hips to the door.

Ivy Lee felt a little lightheaded and nauseous. She sneaked a swallow of homemade wine when she was younger from her father's cup. Van let her have a sip of his beer, but this drink was different. Her hands in the soapy dish water and lost in her thoughts, she heard the screen door slam. Samuel stood holding the empty glass.

"Here you go, gal. I'm all done."

"Ok." She took the glass to the sink and placed it in the soapy water. Before she knew it, Samuel was standing behind her. Her head woozy from the drink.

"Well, I'm leaving and wanted to say goodbye. Can I get a hug?" He pulled Ivy Lee to him with no warning.

"Has anyone ever told you how beautiful you are gal? Whew, when you grow up, you gonna have men falling all over you." Ivy Lee blushed.

"What do you mean when I grow up, I'm not a little girl? I'll be eighteen on my next birthday."

"Eighteen, huh?" Samuel eyeing her figure from top to bottom.

Before Samuel realized it, Ivy Lee moved closer and kissed him, and he didn't resist, but backed up in hesitation. They held each other's gaze while pausing. She seduced him further by unbuttoning her floral cotton dress and let it slip to the floor, as Samuel's eyes widened. She was aware of his reputation, but the curiosity excited her, even though she was a virgin. She knew Samuel was too old for her, and he was family, sort of. Gary never pressured her to be intimate; He was the perfect gentleman. He said they should wait and told her about his dreams for the future which included her. She didn't recognize the feelings she was experiencing with Samuel. It seemed more than the sweet tea, but she lost control in the moment. She grabbed her dress from the floor and tried to cover herself as embarrassment washed over her.

"Gal, have you done this before?" Ivy Lee blushed, but remained silent.

Samuel grasped her hand and led her to the living room. She didn't know what to expect as things advanced, and the initial attention excited her, but she quickly realized this encounter moved beyond what she expected. She pulled away from the discomfort and weight of Samuel on top of her. He paused and asked her if she wanted to stop, but she reassured him, and pretended to enjoy it while she silently waited for it to be over.

Ivy Lee lost track of time and suddenly realized Aunt Dena and Uncle David could return at any moment. She took deep breaths and relaxed and finally let the tension in her body fall away, as Samuel coached her through it.

Ivy Lee awoke in a panic rising from the sofa, frantically fastening her clothes and realizing what took place between her and Samuel, who appeared to have departed. The fleeting womanly feeling had dissipated, and the sheepish country girl was shockingly aware of what transpired. A sudden feeling of shame and sadness washed over her with thoughts of Gary, as tears welled up in her eyes.

The roar of Uncle David's noisy car brought her back to reality. She made sure everything was in place. She remembered the dishes and ran to the kitchen. The dishes were all washed and, in the rack, including the empty mason jar Samuel used, which she didn't remember washing.

The pattern with Samuel repeated itself for the duration of her stay as Samuel became strategic of when Ivy Lee would be alone. She thought Samuel cared for her but knew their interaction was a secret. Samuel was a clever imposter who took advantage of Ivy Lee's gullibility and played on her need for attention, although she gave in willingly. He falsely promised he would try to come to Wadesboro, knowing full well he didn't intend to carry out the promise he made.

***

Ivy Lee said a tearful goodbye to Aunt Dena, Uncle David, and cousin Van as she boarded the bus for the ride back home. Although she missed her parents, she dreaded reuniting with Mabel, and the sad memories of Frank.

Mabel was nice the first night Ivy Lee returned home and was curious about her visit to Raleigh. She noticed her pierced ears as soon as she arrived and made sure Tommie noticed too. Tommie didn't put up a fuss but told Ivy Lee to take care of her ears and she would give her a pair of earrings. Mabel sneered at her, and Ivy Lee knew she returned to the same old Mabel. Ivy Lee didn't share the information about meeting Gary, and surely wouldn't share the experience with Samuel, which she still felt uneasy about, but it made her feel mature.

She quickly settled into her old routine of being intimidated by Mabel and tried to escape the ordinary daily rural life. Since summer ended, she was excited about her final year of high school. She was shy, didn't have any friends, and the boys would taunt her about her well-developed body, which made her appear older than her other female classmates.

Mabel teased Ivy Lee about her increasing weight, over the school year. Tommie, busy with daily life, didn't notice until Mabel brought it to her attention. Ivy Lee was a full-figured teenager, but her looser clothing seemed to strain against her increased weight.

"Ivy Lee, I guess we should go shopping. You need more clothes."

"I know Mama. Mabel keeps teasing me about it, and I don't like it." She responded as she hung her head.

"I will talk to Mabel. You two are sisters." Tommie held out her arms to Ivy Lee. "Give me a hug."

Ivy Lee came over as Tommie stood facing her as they embraced. Tommie felt the bulge in Ivy Lee's stomach and released Ivy Lee quickly falling back. She reached out to feel Ivy Lee's stomach as her mouth fell open.

"Ivy Lee, let me see your stomach, turn to the side!" Ivy Lee obliged as her eyes widened and her head perspired.

"What, Mama, why? What for?" Her voice trembled, and she followed her Mother's request.

"Oh God! You are with child! Ivy Lee!"

"What Mama? No!" Ivy Lee backed away.

"Ivy Lee, have you been having relations?" She repeated as she approached Ivy Lee who turned her back to Tommie.

Ivy Lee kept her eyes to the floor as tears fell. "Yes, Mama." She collapsed in Tommie's arms. Mabel entered the front door and witnessed the two embracing. She dropped her books to the floor and ran over to them.

"Is Daddy ok, what's wrong?"

Ivy Lee ran off to her room leaving Tommie there stunned with disappointment. She didn't know whether she should share the news with Mabel when she was still absorbing it.

"Mabel, Daddy is fine. Everybody is ok, but…" Tommie paused "Ivy Lee is having a baby."

"What? Ivy Lee? Who?" Firing questions one after the other.

"Mabel! I don't know. A baby is coming." Her voice trailing away as she came into the kitchen, still stunned from information revealed from her youngest daughter. It bewildered her on how to break the news to her husband, Johnny.

Mabel ran to the room she and Ivy Lee shared, but Ivy Lee kept her back to the locked door clutching the old skeleton key in her hand. Mabel continued to pound the door while calling out to her.

"Ivy Lee! Let me in! Muffled cries emanated from the closed door. Mabel continued to knock, but with no response. Tommie called Mabel to the kitchen and told her to leave Ivy Lee alone. Mabel hugged a distraught Tommie and asked if she could help her with dinner.

The wrinkles in Tommie's forehead and her tear-filled eyes couldn't hide her feelings. Although her daughters weren't aware, Tommie became pregnant when she was a teen, forced to give her baby to a distant aunt who was barren. She never stopped thinking about her first son, who she wasn't allowed to name, but she never forgot about him. She didn't even know where they lived. Her Mother told her to forget about him, and she couldn't tell anyone including the baby's father. Every year on September seventeenth, she would remember him and say a prayer. She hoped for a reunion and vowed to never forget him.

Tommie was a quiet, God-fearing hard-working woman who never complained. Her worn hands ached from years of laundry and scarred from the short time she picked cotton alongside of her sisters. Her father told her he didn't want his daughters in those cotton fields. Meeting Johnny was the best thing from her time in the fields. She was shy and ignored his attention at first, but her sisters encouraged her, and after a short courtship, they married and moved to Wadesboro. She wanted a family, and when her son, the middle child was born, she gave him the name Frank, which she picked out for her first son. Frank could do no wrong; He got away with a lot. Losing Frank took its toll on her; she endured the loss of another son.

Ivy Lee came out of her room after dark. Tommie sat folding clothes, Mabel reading, and her father Johnny asleep in the chair.

Tommy summoned Ivy Lee over to her and held her hands in hers. "Ivy Lee, we will get through this. We're disappointed, but we will help you. Sit down and eat. You need to see a doctor. When was

77

your last monthly?" Mabel lowered her book and glanced over at Ivy Lee. Ivy Lee shot Mabel an angry glare.

"I don't remember Mama. I don't know, I'm sorry." She lowered her eyes to the ground.

"Ivy Lee, who is the father? He needs to provide for this baby. Is he going to marry you? Your Daddy may need to go speak to his folks."

"I will take care of my baby, Mama. I can get a job. I don't want to talk about it anymore, please don't make me." Ivy Lee wept. Her sobs woke up her father, who stood up rubbing his eyes.

"Ivy Lee! Come over here chile. Why are you crying? I know about it. I'm disappointed, but this baby is family, and we'll find a way." Ivy Lee buried her face in his chest as he hugged her. Mabel rolled her eyes as she witnessed their interaction. She felt Ivy Lee was his favorite.

The visit to the doctor revealed Ivy Lee was due in a matter of weeks. Tommie stunned, but tried to hide her reaction from Ivy Lee. She notified the local granny-midwife who delivered all her children at home.

***

After many hours of labor on this early May morning, Ivy Lee delivered a beautiful baby boy. She was so exhausted; she could barely stay awake to meet him. Johnny brought in the crib used by all his children, including Georgia. Mabel was attentive to Ivy Lee during labor, encouraging her to push when she couldn't gather any energy and wiped the sweat from her forehead. Tommie handed the baby over to Mabel who rocked him with tear-filled eyes before gently placing him in the bassinet. Mabel wiped away tears. "He's beautiful." She tended to Ivy Lee who was sleeping soundly. Seeing her two daughters brought Tommie joy; It was rare that they were not at odds.

Ivy Lee couldn't rest; her new little baby needed to eat. The granny-midwife left, and Tommie and Mabel showed a nervous Ivy

Lee how to breast feed her little one. He latched on quickly. She put on a brave face despite being overwhelmed.

Mabel gazed down at the tiny infant Ivy Lee named Riley as he slept. Thumb in his mouth and his other hand in his fine curly hair. This moment brought back sad thoughts of Georgia.

Guilt would visit Mabel often during the month of August. As much as she tried, she couldn't bury it. No one blamed her for what happened, but she couldn't bring Georgia back. Tommie's screams still echoed and haunted her during quiet moments. No one ever knew how much baby meant to her and the deep connection they shared. *I will never forget her eyes, his eyes.* she thought.

Chapter 19

Rebound

"Good morning, Mrs. Patterson! It's Nurse Emily. I'm so thrilled to see you up and out of bed. How are you feeling?"

"I feel much better, and I'm so hungry."

Ivy Lee peered through the security grate covering the window. The sun was shining, and the sky was a beautiful clear blue. She wasn't shaking, her mind felt clear, and her words were no longer slurred.

"Breakfast will arrive soon, and Dr. Timmons should be here after that." Nurse Emily watched Ivy Lee take her medicine.

"Thank you." Ivy Lee placed the tiny, white pleated paper cup back on the tray Nurse Emily was holding.

Ivy Lee ate everything on her food tray. Her energy was still quite low, but at least she felt motivated to shower and dress. She couldn't wait to speak to Dr. Timmons to tell him how good she felt.

Dr. Timmons knocked on the door while poking his head in. "Mrs. Patterson, may I come in?"

"Yes, please come in."

"How are you feeling?"

"I feel much better, Dr. Timmons."

"The nurse told me you ate all of your breakfast! I'm pleased. It took time for you to respond to the medicine. You should be able to go home in a couple of days, but it's important you stay consistent when taking the medicine which I am prescribing you. It won't be effective if you don't. I will review it with Mr.Patterson so you both understand the regimen. I have diagnosed you as having a manic-depressive disorder." Ivy Lee's eyes widened with confusion as Dr. Timmons took her hand.

"When you experience a period of extreme energy, it's the illness. Then sometimes you feel sad for no reason and depressed like a dark cloud is following you, your energy is low, and you can hardly function. Both are part of the disorder. There are highs and lows. The medicine I am prescribing for you, lithium salts, will help to level off those emotions. Do you understand?"

"Yes, I do. Will I need it all the time? I don't like feeling drowsy."

"Yes, Mrs. Patterson, it's important to keep to a regular schedule. If you don't, you'll experience more of those highs and lows."

"Ok. I think I understand. Thank you, Dr. Timmons."

"I spoke to Mr. Patterson earlier and updated him how you were doing. He said he will come see you this afternoon.

"My Willie! I can't wait to see him!"

"Believe me, he is excited to see you as well."

The swift opening of the hospital door brought with it a sudden breeze.

"Willie!" Ivy Lee squealed.

Ivy Lee leaped off the bed and nearly lost her balance. Willie caught her by her elbow to steady her.

Dr. Timmons watched the two of them embrace. "Hello, Mr. Patterson!"

"Oh hello, Dr. Timmons. I didn't see you there."

"It's all right, Mr. Patterson. I'm happy to see her up and I'm sure you are too."

"I sure am!" Willie squeezed Ivy Lee tight to him as they sat down on her hospital bed.

"We need to be careful. Sometimes the initial improvement during leveling off the medicine is short lived."

Willie went from elation to disappointment. "I don't understand, Dr. Timmons."

"Well Mr. Patterson, sometimes a patient will feel like they can jump back into situations, where they were uncomfortable before. You must approach them slowly. The medication is no cure but keeps Ivy Lee at a level of normal functioning. Some patients experience initial side effects: nausea, headaches, possible diarrhea, and I know you have already experienced some hand tremors. We are hoping over time, these effects will subside."

"Ok, I know what you mean."

Dr. Timmons tone serious. "Ivy Lee, do you understand?"

"Yes, I think so."

"Also, certain people, locations, or situations can trigger an episode, which you call a spell, even while you are taking the medication. We will continue your therapy to work through what you are feeling and monitor how the medication affects you. I'm pleased with how this regimen is working and your progress so far. The administrator will prepare the paperwork for your release, and I'll see you in two weeks. Questions for me?" Ivy Lee stood and extended her hand to Dr. Timmons.

"Thank you." Dr. Timmons patted her hand and turned to leave after giving Willie a firm handshake. "Thank you, Dr. Timmons, I will take good care of her."

"I don't doubt it, Mr. Patterson."

Chapter 20

Home

Willie and Ivy Lee wanted a home of their own. One of Willie's coworkers, Jimmy, told him about the house he was trying to sell which belonged to his late mother. It was a small two-bedroom brick house on the west side of Detroit. Jimmy and Willie worked together on the garbage truck route for the last five years. Jimmy trusted Willie and gave him the keys to take Ivy Lee to see it. Willie could barely contain his excitement. Jimmy was asking $10,000 for the house. Willie was frugal and had been secretly saving for a house. He decided he would go by and see it first.

As he pulled up to the small brick bungalow, he noticed how manicured the lush green lawn was. He loved doing yard work and relished at the thought of making this house their home. Before he approached the front porch, he went around to the backyard. As he lifted the latch to the gate leading to the backyard, his eyes lit up. The borders of the yard were in bloom with beautiful flowers of every hue. Next to the one-car garage was a sectioned off area, which appeared to be a vegetable garden. Although overgrown with weeds, he could see the potential. Ivy Lee loved flowers; It would thrill her at the prospect of a garden. He stepped on the stony grass covered trail, which led to a cemented path to the side door. He turned the rusty lock several times before it would release and allow the door to open. The damp smell of the unfinished basement hit his nostrils. He took the two steps which led to the tiny kitchen neatly decorated with wallpaper from its ceiling to the wooden baseboard. The vinyl linoleum floor was dingy and buckled near the edges, but he knew Ivy Lee would love the speckled Formica countertops. *God sent this opportunity*, he thought, and couldn't wait to tell Ivy Lee about it. He imagined the tasty meals she would prepare in this kitchen.

***

As Willie opened the apartment door, he could smell the familiar scent of Ivy Lee's delicious meatloaf. He knew what was in store for him: mashed potatoes, gravy, peas, and freshly baked cornbread; one of his favorite meals.

"Hey honey! How was your day? I see you have been cooking my favorites."

"Yes, I made meatloaf, and peach cobbler for dessert."

"Oh, my goodness!"

Ivy Lee took off her flowered apron and threw it over the back of the kitchen chair. They embraced for a moment and shared a deep passionate kiss. Ivy Lee felt Willie's hand slyly travel down to squeeze her full hips, and she let out a shy giggle.

"Oh Willie, are you getting fresh with me?"

"You know me well darling, but first I have something exciting to tell you. Let's sit down." He said while grasping Ivy Lee's hands in his.

"Baby, you know how we have wanted a house of our own, well Jimmy is selling his mother's house. You remember she died about six months ago. I've seen it, but I want us to go after dinner so you can see it. I have already fallen in love with it, and I hope you do too."

"Oh, Willie! I'm so excited! Let's eat!"

Willie and Ivy Lee enjoyed the delicious meal. It was hard for them to contain their enthusiasm. Ivy Lee washed up the dinner dishes and grabbed her purse and sweater. Willie was already backing the car out of the parking space and pulled in front of the apartment walkway to wait for Ivy Lee. The house was a short ten-minute drive away.

As they turned the corner, Willie pointed out the small brick house. A big smile spread across her face as he pulled into the driveway. She patiently waited until he came around and opened the passenger door. As they approached the front porch, Ivy Lee stopped to survey the neighborhood of manicured lawns and well-kept dwellings. She could picture herself in this setting. The house was small but cozy. Jimmy left furniture in the house he said they were welcome to keep if they bought it. Ivy Lee went into the tiny kitchen which felt perfect for her. She began thinking of the curtains she would make for the kitchen windows which faced the front of the house. The kitchen and other rooms needed a fresh coat of paint.

"Willie, I love it! I love the kitchen; I love it all! Can we afford to buy it, baby?"

"Yes, Dear! I saved up a down payment. I love our apartment, but this, this we could call home." Ivy Lee teared up and ambled over to Willie hugging him tightly.

"Thank you, Willie." Her head buried against his chest muffling her sobs.

"I know those are happy tears baby, let them out. I'm happy too."

They returned to their apartment and planned to speak with Jimmy in the morning to convey their desire to purchase the property. It was perfect timing since their apartment's lease was up for renewal at the end of next month. Willie contacted his bank to pursue a mortgage, so he was confident everything was in place and couldn't wait to move into their new home. Ivy Lee spent the next month packing and throwing away old items. She saved a few of the toys from when Riley was younger.

When the first of the next month arrived, Willie borrowed a coworker's truck and a couple of other coworkers helped move their belongings to their new home. Ivy Lee was already there putting up curtains she made for the kitchen and bathroom. She pulled out a new spread to put on their bed once they assembled it. They planned to find a bed for the extra room when Riley stayed over. Mabel was still upset about the baptism and wouldn't let Riley visit. Once, they settled in, Ivy Lee planned to call her and invite them over for dinner.

She hoped this would soften Mabel, so they could get back to communicating. *At least Riley still called and told Ivy Lee he missed and loved her*, she thought.

***

Ivy Lee worked nonstop getting the house ready. She had Ida Mae over for tea before inviting Mabel, but she planned to invite Mabel and Riley to a fish fry the coming Friday. They enjoyed catching up. Ida Mae took some slices of pound cake home to share with Big Joe. She also shared the secret with Ivy Lee she may be pregnant but was waiting to see the doctor to confirm it. She gushed about having all the signs: two missed periods, nausea, and dizziness; all signs she could be expecting. Ivy Lee was ecstatic but envious and shared her excitement with Ida Mae. She and Willie tried for years, but when she began taking medication for the depression, her doctors advised her against it. She knew Mabel would behave in the presence of Randall and Riley. Willie found a nice twin bed and matching dresser for the spare room and painted the walls with light blue paint. Ivy Lee hoped Mabel would let Riley stay over soon but didn't want to get her hopes up.

Ivy Lee was glad to have Ida Mae to confide in. Ida Mae listened as Ivy Lee described her distressing hospital experience. Ida Mae encouraged her to keep taking her medicine and promised to get together more often. The two were as close as sisters. Ivy Lee's relationship with Mabel was more of a domineering parent criticizing a child. She loved Mabel but braced herself for an impending attack. As she watched Ida Mae depart, she glanced around the living room and kitchen, taking it all in. She felt happy and so grateful for this moment of peace, clarity, and love.

Chapter 21

Fish Fry

"Hello?"

"Good morning, Mabel!"

"Hi Ivy Lee, how are you?"

"I feel good. I'm taking my medicine, and I feel much better."

"You sound good."

" I would like to invite you all for a fish fry this Friday. Are you all available?"

"Yes, we are. I can't wait to see your new home. What time should we be there?"

"How about 6:30?"

"6:30 is perfect."

"See you then, Sister."

Ivy Lee prayed as she hung up the phone; she wanted everything to be perfect on Friday.

The week went by quickly. Ivy Lee glanced at the red clock shaped like an apple on the kitchen wall and heard the doorbell ring. She stood and took a deep breath before opening the door. She could see Mabel, Randall, and Riley through the full-length glass door covered with white curtain sheers. Mabel carried a wrapped package under her arm. As Ivy Lee opened the door, Willie joined her and placed his palm on her back. He knew how nervous she was, and he was supportive as usual. Mabel gave Ivy Lee a long tight hug. Ivy Lee couldn't recall the last time they embraced this way. It felt good. She handed Ivy Lee the beautiful box wrapped in shiny gold paper with a giant bow on top.

"This is for your new home Sister. I hope you like it."

"Thank you!"

"Go ahead, open it."

Ivy Lee sat down and excitedly unwrapped the package. Wrapped in gold tissue paper was a crystal frame with a picture of their parents sitting on the front porch back in Wadesboro. Ivy Lee teared up.

"Thank you, Mabel, I love it! It brings back so many wonderful memories. Their father, Johnny, was sitting in the worn wicker chair with a corn pipe sticking out of his mouth dressed in the only suit he owned. Tommie was standing next to him with a big fine hat, and a sleeveless dress, black pumps, and white gloves. Even though the photograph was in black and white, Ivy Lee vividly remembers Tommie's favorite dress was navy blue with white polka dots. She rarely found the occasion to dress up. She closed her eyes as she recalled the flowery scent of her mother's perfume.

Ivy Lee wiped away her tears kissed Mabel on the cheek. Willie and Randall, smiling stood by and observed this rare interaction. Riley came and grabbed Ivy Lee tightly around her waist. Ivy Lee covered Riley's face with kisses and showed him the extra room, which was all set for him. She was careful not to say it was his room, but they clearly filled it with all kinds of toys he would love.

Chapter 22

Ivy Lee's Garden

The sound of a lawnmower buzzing in the background awakened Ivy Lee. She noticed Willie was already out of the bed and peeked through curtain sheers in the window facing the backyard to see him mowing the lawn, *I better get up and fix him something to eat* she thought.

A couple of hours later after breakfast, and some light house cleaning, Willie backed the car out so they could head down to the Eastern Market, a farmer's Market in Midtown on Russell Street. Mabel took them there upon their arrival in Detroit. The sheds were stocked with fresh fruits, vegetables, and flowers. There were also a couple of meat markets, which were staples there. Ivy Lee was interested in purchasing some tomato plants, squash, collard greens, and cucumbers to sow her garden whose soil was carefully tilled by Willie.

After returning from the farmer's market, Willie got Ivy Lee settled with a chair out in the garden and handed her the big new straw hat she found at a flea market. He reminded her not to overdo it. "Don't stay out in this heat too long, Ivy Lee." She nodded.

The sun made her feel good. She missed the southern temperatures, but she didn't miss the humid Florida air.

"I won't. I'll be napping by the time you come back."

"Here's some ice water," he announced as he kissed her on the forehead and left.

Ivy Lee diligently planted each small seedling in the moist earth while humming. After laying the tools beside the garage she stood and marvelled at the neat rows of vegetables before her; She was proud of her work. Once back inside, she took her medicine, a long bath, and napped in the spare room. As she surveyed the room filled with toys, she didn't feel sadness, but felt joy at the possibility of Riley spending the night. She wanted to give him everything. The gifts she gave Riley at Christmas and Easter were her way of showing love, but the time spent with him was priceless. Each time he left was difficult, but she was patient until their next visit.

The weekend ended with a wonderful meal at one of the Deacon's houses. The Malones were not privy to Ivy Lee's condition. They were the sweetest couple and childless, with many infertility struggles and sadly a still birth. Tessa and Ivy Lee instantly bonded. Tessa, who was born in Detroit marveled at the stories Ivy Lee would tell about the south and southern traditions.

When they returned home and were getting ready for bed, Ivy Lee stumbled slightly while putting on her nightgown.

"Baby, are you, all right?"

"I'm ok, felt a little dizzy is all."

"Did you take your medicine?"

"Yes, I did. It's been a long day, I'm just tired."

"Ok, get some rest, I'm going to get my work clothes ready, but I'll be in bed soon."

"Ok, Willie."

Ivy Lee nervously pulled back the covers and lay down on the cool sheets and drifted off to sleep. Shortly thereafter, Willie slid into bed, so as not to disturb her. He faced her back and said a prayer for his wife before falling asleep.

The next morning Ivy Lee woke up to the melody of chirping birds and the sun peeking through the beige drapes. A coffee cup, saucer and knife with remnants of butter and jelly lay in the sink.

A typical weekday began, for Ivy Lee, but this time the garden was her focus. After getting dressed, she went out to water her garden.

The smell of the wet soil combined with the sun on her face, brought joy to her spirit.

Chapter 23

Sleepover

"**M**om?"

"Yes, Riley."

"May I go spend the weekend with Auntie? I really like her church."

"You do baby? What do you like about it?"

"The people and the singing."

"It's ok with me. Let's check with her first."

Riley ran and gave her a quick hug and then ran to the telephone on the end table. He was so excited; he could hardly keep his fingers steady to dial the rotary phone. A big smile lit up his face.

"Hello!"

"Hi Auntie! How are you and Uncle Willie?"

"Oh, we are fine. I have been working in my new garden."

"Auntie, may I come over on Saturday and go to church with you?"

"Yes! Did you ask your Mother if it was ok?

"Yes, she is right here. Do you want to speak with her?"

"Yes, I do."

Riley excitedly handed the telephone to Mabel.

"Hi, Sister, how are you?"

"Hi Mabel, I'm fine!"

"I'm so excited to spend time with Riley. Thank You."

"What time is good for you?"

"How about four o'clock?"

"Four o'clock is fine, I'll bring him by then. See you soon."

"Ok Sister, I will see you soon. Bye."

Riley hugged Mabel again and ran to his room to pack.

Upon arrival at Ivy Lee's home, she was already standing in the doorway displaying a big smile in her favorite flowered apron.

"Hi Sister! Come on in!" As Mabel exited the car, she marveled at the beautiful houses on the block.

"This is a pretty neighborhood, Ivy Lee."

"I fell in love with it the first day we saw it. Do you want to see my garden?"

"Oh yes, I would love to see it!" The narrow sidewalk on the side of the house led to the tidy backyard.

"Oh, Ivy Lee! This is nice!"

"Thank you! I've planted tomatoes, squash, cucumbers and collards."

"I love squash!" Riley squealed. They laughed and headed towards the side door.

"It smells wonderful in here!"

"Yes, I cooked all of Riley's favorites."

"It's so sweet of you, Ivy Lee." Mabel hugged her.

"Ivy Lee, you look well. I'm so proud of you."

"Thank you for allowing me to spend some time with my nephew."

"I need to apologize for how I've been acting. I can see the love between you and Riley. Enjoy your visit. Will Willie be able to drop him off after church?"

"Yes! Willie will bring him home." Riley kissed Mabel on the cheek and hurried back to the spare bedroom. Ivy Lee watched as Mabel backed her new Chevy out of the driveway. She felt relieved and surprised at Mabel's pleasant disposition, but hoped it would continue. She vowed not to cross boundaries with Riley which could affect her spending more time with him.

After Ivy Lee got Riley settled in bed, she retreated to her favorite chair and watched the Jackie Gleason show until she felt tired and roused a sleeping Willie and convinced him to get in bed. Hours later, a crying Riley awakened them.

"Auntie! Auntie!" screamed Riley as he barreled into their bedroom as they slept in on this lazy Saturday morning.

"What's the matter, Riley?" She leaped from her bed.

"I had a bad dream, it seemed so real." Riley screamed "It was so real, Mama died!" Ivy Lee was worried he would hyperventilate; his eyes fixed as if he were half- asleep.

"It's ok, Riley, it was only a dream. Your Mother is fine, baby." She hugged Riley. He was trembling. "Do you want to call her, I'm sure she's up?"

"Yes, Auntie, can I please?"

It's going to be okay, baby. I promise you it will." She grabbed the telephone and sat it on the dining room table while holding Riley's hand. Ivy Lee dialed and told Mabel what happened. She handed the receiver to Riley, and although she couldn't hear the conversation on the other end, she could tell whatever Mabel was saying soothed him. He appeared calmer and handed the phone back to Ivy Lee.

"Hi Sister, he seems ok now."

"Ivy Lee, thanks for calling me. He has nightmares, although it's been a long time. It terrifies him. It's normally about different things, but he seems to have frequent dreams of seeing close family members die."

"He's scared, and I knew speaking with you would calm him down. I love him so much."

"Yes, I know you and Willie love and take excellent care of him. He'll be all right, don't worry."

"I won't." As they hung up, Mabel was proud of the way Ivy Lee handled Riley.

With all of Ivy Lee's issues, she embodied a loving caring spirit. The rest of the day remained uneventful.

"Riley, would you like to join me? I bought some new coloring books I think you will like."

"Yes! You make the pictures so pretty."

Coloring was one thing Ivy Lee enjoyed. She would combine different colors and blend them with a tissue. They sat huddled on the couch together for a couple of hours until Riley said he was hungry. Ivy Lee made him a peanut butter and jelly sandwich, with a glass of milk.

Willie arrived home after dropping Ivy Lee and Riley off at home earlier returning to church for a meeting. He marveled at the sight of them snuggled up on the couch. Ivy Lee read to him as he endearingly lay his head on her shoulder. His gaze jumping between the page and gazing lovingly at her; the sweetest vision.

"I had the best time, Auntie! I can't wait to come back and visit again."

"I love you baby, take care." She gave him a hug and closed her eyes to savor the moment. Ivy Lee watched as Riley hopped in the back seat, with his new coloring book tucked under his arm, and the little stuffed animal monkey, she found at the secondhand store. It reminded her of the favorite childhood toy she cherished given to her by her grandma. Her grandma kept it at the top of the closet and would let her play with it when she came to visit. She let Riley take his stuffed toy home.

When Willie returned, Ivy Lee was taking a relaxing bath while his dinner was being kept warm in the oven. As he knocked and peeked in, he could see Ivy Lee's eyes closed as she smiled. She wasn't asleep, but appeared serene. Not wanting to disturb her, he sat down to read the newspaper. He knew Riley's visit made her happy. He'd kept track of her medicine. Her stable behavior coincided with it which relieved him.

A warm kiss awakened Willie while napping in the overstuffed living room chair followed by a soft caress on his neck. His eyes still closed, he inhaled the familiar scent of her favorite perfume, and opened his eyes to see her wearing a long blue nylon nightgown and her bare feet as she grasped Willie's hand, as he rose from the chair. Ivy Lee exhaled as they embraced. When they broke their embrace, their eyes locked in a loving gaze, with no words spoken. She felt content, safe, and in sound mind; three things she longed for. An exhausted Willie turned off the living room lamp and followed Ivy Lee into the bedroom. He let the day flow away from him as Ivy Lee massaged his back until he drifted off to sleep. Even though he craved the intimacy lacking between them, she seemed to know exactly what he needed in this moment.

Ivy Lee's mental health traveled through peaks and valleys over the next months, and she endured the occasional nightmare, where she would wake up screaming and jump up in fear frantically searching for a baby, which worried Willie. It took him at least an hour or two to calm her during these episodes and convince her she didn't lose a baby. The next morning, she would wake and have no memory of the previous night.

Chapter 24

The Dark Cloud Returns

Although the sun was shining, Ivy Lee felt like a dark cloud was consuming her. She remembered Willie saying he would be home late because it was his turn to cover someone's shift. She remained in bed for two consecutive days. The meal Willie brought her before he left for work hours ago, grew cold. She couldn't shake this down feeling. Willie suggested she go see Dr. Timmons again, but Ivy Lee remembered the last experience where they kept her overnight. It was horrible. She recalled being put in a room, and before she knew it, they gave her an injection, and she awoke the next morning not being able to remember anything but laying on the hard metal bed with her arms in leather restraints. Her vision was hazy, as she went in and out of consciousness. She couldn't recall speaking with anyone, but vividly remembered hearing moans and screams from the corridor.

Hours later, Ivy Lee woke up in the corner of the dark damp basement sweating profusely, and naked. The icy chill of the dank basement floor shocked her bare skin as she regained consciousness.

"Where am I? Willie! Willie!" She screamed as she grabbed her knees to her exposed chest realizing she was naked on the cold basement floor. A streak of sunshine crept through the torn shade of the southern basement window. A spider crawled down an invisible web near her left side, and she squealed.

"I can't move!"

The stench of urine wafted up to her nose, and she felt the wetness of her inner thighs. Embarrassment washed over her. She tried to steady herself as she placed her knuckles on the cement floor to brace herself as she tried to stand. With one arm across her breasts, her other arm unsuccessfully covered the rest of her unclothed body, shielding her nakedness even though there was no one around. Her eyes focused in the dimly lit basement where her eyes searched for the stairwell. The cold cement shocking the soles of her bare feet. Each step creaked, and she felt the rough worn wood beneath her feet as she moved to the door which led to the kitchen.

"What time is it? Where are my clothes?"

When she entered the kitchen, she saw her nightgown by the entrance to the living room. The front door wasn't open enough to see inside. Every room was in disarray. It appeared as if someone threw a tantrum and tossed everything around the room. Ivy Lee fell to the carpeted floor onto a pile of newspapers and wept so hard she could hardly breathe. Glimmers of the day crept into her memory, and she understood the madness which occurred in her home was of her own doing. She vaguely remembered her ears ringing and covering her ears and crouching in a corner of the living room. She didn't even recollect making her way back upstairs and into bed, but the sound of the dripping water still echoed in her ears. "I know I need help, but I cannot go back in there. I can't let Willie see our beautiful home like this. He'll know."

She rushed and tried to put everything in its place, dreading the hours she would be alone. She again sobbed uncontrollably with mascara running down her face which was smeared with makeup she couldn't remember applying. She rambled over and over, "I need help!" Ivy Lee realized she could no longer avoid the madness which had become her life. Everything was so foggy, but one thing was clear, she needed to seek treatment again. Each episode more frightening than the last. As the sun set, Ivy Lee could hear Willie coming in the front door. The sound of his keys startled her.

"I'm home. Did you eat?" He entered the bedroom. Ivy Lee was facing away and as he got closer, he could see the uneaten tray of food he left her.

"Baby you've got to eat something, so you can take your medicine." Willie saw her tear-stained face.

"What's wrong, why are you crying?" Kissing her sweaty forehead.

"I don't know, Willie, I don't know."

"You'll be alright, my love."

Willie leaned down and embraced Ivy Lee, which seemed to diffuse her distress. She neglected to share with Willie about awakening in the basement because she knew it would make him worry more. She finally relaxed as Willie comforted her, but she was fearful for what the next day would bring when she was alone again.

Ivy Lee stayed shuttered in her room for days. As much as she enjoyed watching her soap operas, she didn't go into the living room to turn on the television. She felt afraid and the incident in the basement unnerved her. The dark cloud lifted somewhat, and at least she felt like getting up and getting dressed. She hadn't felt hungry in days.

It seemed like forever since Riley's visit, but it was only a few weeks ago. When the dim cloud enveloped her, she lost track of time. This spell seemed different; she couldn't shake it. Consumed by this dark place, the overall feeling of dread and the sudden wave of depression tormented her.

She remembered Willie leaving, but typically he left something for her to eat. He left a tray on the kitchen table. Under the covered plate were two boiled eggs, a slice of toast, and slices of bacon. Ivy Lee started the oven and reheated her bacon and toast. The percolator was full but unplugged. It warmed quickly, and the familiar aromatic scent of coffee filled the air. All at once, she remembered Sonny. She ran to his cage and discovered Willie already fed him. She opened his cage and he quickly exited and perched atop a corner bookshelf. Willie was never fond of this practice but allowed her to do it occasionally. *I'm so lucky to have found Willie*, she thought. *He's such a good man.* She

99

reminisced about their first meeting at church in Jacksonville. He told Ivy Lee he couldn't remember the sermon, but he remembered her.

Ivy Lee felt better after eating. She took a long bath and cooked dinner. She put Sonny back in his cage so she wouldn't forget before Willie got home. He arrived surprised but relieved to see her out of bed.

"Everything is delicious, but the best thing is seeing you feel better."

"I don't mean to worry you, but it comes over me, and I try to shake it, but it takes all my energy. You're so patient with me."

Willie contemplated what they went through. The first time her mood and personality changes occurred were within their first few months of dating. After spending a full day together, a shopping trip and lunch, they planned to see a movie later in the evening. Ivy Lee relaxed, smiling and laughing at Willie's jokes when he dropped her off earlier. When Willie arrived to pick her up for the movie later, it took ten minutes for her to answer the door. She opened the door a small crack revealing her red puffy eyes. She wanted to know why he came. He left confused and worried. It surprised him to see her this way especially after they spent the entire day together where she seemed to be full of energy and looked forward to their date. The next morning when he called, she appeared to him to be her same lively self and couldn't wait to see him later for the movie he promised to take her to. Willie questioned her if she remembered him coming by the night before to pick her up, and she said she remembered being dropped off, and he must have his days mixed up. Willie hung up the phone and tried to shrug it off. When he arrived, she was waiting at the door excited about their date. Many months went by before he noticed any more of her unusual behavior.

Willie's Mother, Ann, adored Ivy Lee. Ann stricken with debilitating rheumatoid arthritis, struggled to get around. Ivy Lee loved to visit and was attentive to her, cooked her favorite dishes and platted her long thick wavy black hair. The two of them became close. Ivy Lee was the daughter she prayed for. When they married, they moved in to help. Sadly, she died unexpectedly after suffering a heart attack a month after. They were both devastated. Ann reminded Ivy Lee of Tommie; quiet, strong, and loving.

His mind drifted back to a recent time when Ivy Lee led him into the bedroom. He couldn't remember the last time they were intimate. He stopped pursuing it but missed the affection they once regularly shared. The dimly lit room silhouetted the curves of Ivy Lee's voluptuous body, as she let her sheer teal satin nightgown drop to the floor. A captivated Willie allowed Ivy Lee to seduce him. She never initiated their encounters, but he relaxed and enjoyed this rare moment.

The next morning Willie overslept and awoke to the aroma of hickory bacon cooking. At first, he jumped up, thinking he was late for work, but realized it was Saturday morning. He made his way to the kitchen to see Ivy Lee, dressed in the teal nightgown and matching robe and humming softly as she placed each utensil on the table. Willie came up behind her pressing his body against hers and kissing her on the neck. Ivy Lee turned around and hugged him as they shared a passionate kiss. Willie grinned. "I enjoyed last night, Ivy Lee."

"I did too. Are you ready for breakfast?" She beamed.

"Yes, baby, I'm starving." He sat down at the table.

Ivy Lee joined Willie at the table as they said grace and ate their meal in between their flirting and blushing from their night together.

"Would you like to go shopping today? Mother's Day is coming up and I would love to buy you a new dress."

"I would love it. Let's go to Crowley's. I think there's a sale."

"Are you singing in the program?"

"Yes, one song. They said it was my choice, but I haven't decided what I'm going to sing yet."

"Whatever you decide, it will be beautiful, baby."

Willie put his dishes in the sink and headed towards the bathroom to shave and get ready to take Ivy Lee shopping. He was so excited, reminiscent of time before the spells.

***

Ivy Lee's garden died out with the season's change, and she felt stifled by the end of her daily routine. Even though she occasionally enjoyed her paint by number set, she lost interest. A few months after they moved to their new home, she woke up to discover her beloved parakeet Sonny's lifeless body lying at the bottom on the cage. When Willie arrived home, he convinced Ivy Lee to bury Sonny near her garden. A small hat box in her closet, lined with cheese cloth, was used to bury her precious Sonny in the shallow hole Willie dug near the fence. After crying for three days straight, she mustered up the energy to plant tulip bulbs over the spot as a beautiful reminder of Sonny. Willie tried to convince her to get another bird, but she said no bird could replace Sonny.

Chapter 25

Lost

Ivy Lee woke up nervous this cold fall morning. She searched frantically through old purses but couldn't find even one cigarette. She'd never ventured out in the neighborhood before, but craved a cigarette so bad she put on her winter coat over her duster and flimsy house shoes on her feet and headed out to the corner store. When she got to the counter, she realized she forgot to bring money. Distraught, she headed towards the exit and was met by an usher from her church. Embarrassed being seen this way, she lowered her head and quickened her steps towards the door.

"Sister Patterson! Sister Patterson!" She stood in the brisk wind waiting for the light to change. "Do you need a ride?"

"I need a cigarette!" Her hands trembled. "You have one?"

"Sure. You shouldn't be out here. It's freezing."

Ivy Lee, turned around, as she pulled her coat tighter. Not dressed for the extreme cold that shocked her body, she quickly realized her clothing was inadequate for the weather. She nodded and acknowledged she would accept a ride home. She got in the passenger side and stayed silent for the short ride home. He handed her a cigarette and lit it for her. He pulled into her driveway, and she got out before he put the car in park.

"Thank you." She rushed into the house and pushed the front door closed.

She forgot to lock the door and take her keys when she left. Still craving another cigarette, she rifled through a bedroom drawer to find enough change. She fell to the bed after she got dizzy. Sweat poured from her body. The swirling in her head and rapid heartbeat overcame her.

Hours later she woke up in the dark basement and lost track of time again. It unnerved her when she found herself down there again. Her puffy eyes heavy. A constant drip echoed from the dark corner near where she could see a shadow of the cement sink, and a streak of light peeked through the torn rust-stained shade. This scenario seemed to repeat itself. She didn't remember going to the basement. The dank musty scent pierced her nostrils and goosebumps covered her naked frame. Her bare back felt frozen to the concrete dampened by the leaky water pipes. She didn't like coming down the basement to do laundry, but kept finding herself there. Her damp ankles brought back the memory of being in the wet muddy corn fields the night Georgia died.

Droplets of cold moisture seeped into her matted hair like a slow murky rainstorm. An invisible weight of dread pinned her in the cobwebbed filled corner, as she tried to use her hands to push up from the chilly floor, but she fell against the wall. The shock of the brick wall hitting her head stunned her, and she struggled to steady herself. She stood and gazed down at her nude body shielding her bare breasts with one arm and the other covering her wet pubic hair. She realized the cold wetness running down her legs to her knees. Glimpses flashed through her memory as she made her way back upstairs. When she returned to the living room, the door was partially closed. She noticed a watch wedged at the bottom of the door. She didn't recognize it as belonging to Willie nor did she remember seeing it there before. As she picked it up, the memory of an intimate encounter came flooding back. *It's not real,* she thought. She couldn't picture his face at all. The last thing she remembered was coming back home after trying to purchase cigarettes. She realized the wetness were the remnants of an intimate encounter she couldn't recall.

This isn't real, she thought. "If only the watch wasn't there. Why does this keep happening? I love Willie," the thought terrified her. As she picked up her duster from the floor, it held a hint of a man's cologne. Her heart raced, and she realized this was yet another episode. Suddenly she envisioned speaking to the usher as he banged on the door. She vaguely remembers inviting him in, but the flirting between them became clear. The large metal clock on the living room wall revealing hours had passed and it would still be several hours before Willie arrived home.

Still craving a cigarette, she cleaned herself up and attempted another trip before it got dark. As she waited for the light to change, the environment around her felt like it was swirling, and her vision became hazy. She couldn't remember which direction she came from. She could scarcely make out the green light to cross the street, but the spinning continued. In between the spiraling she felt in her head, she kept seeing visions of the intimate encounter between her and the usher whose name she couldn't remember. It was then she realized she started the encounter, but it made little sense to her. She barely interacted with him in church. The thought sickened her.

She couldn't see the store or the way home. It was getting dark, and the bitter stiff wind was howling through her thin garments. Ivy Lee scared, but she took a deep breath, and leaned on a light pole to get her bearings, closing her eyes momentarily, and whispering a prayer. Finally, the dizziness subsided, and she headed in the direction which she thought would take her home. She crossed at the light she believed was toward her block, and nausea came over her, and she vomited on the curb, heaving until nearly passing out. She felt weak and her forehead was sweaty, but she continued hiking, which seemed like blocks. No open businesses were in view. She faintly saw the light of a gas station, through the blizzard. By this time, she was freezing, her feet and limbs felt like icy blocks, but she continued to make her way towards the hazy light of the gas station. When she reached the station to get warm before seeking the right direction to go in, she noticed an empty police car parked near the entrance. Feeling disoriented, she stumbled into the station, and leaned against the metal candy dispensers by the door. The rattling gumballs hitting against the glass made both officers turn around in unison.

The taller of the two burly white police officers approached her. "Miss, are you, all right? Are you waiting for someone?"

"No, I kind of got turned around. I'm new to the neighborhood. I went to the store and lost my way." Ivy Lee fainted. The two officers grabbed her by each arm and the gas station attendant dragged over a chair for her to sit down.

"Ma'am, can we take you to the hospital? Is there someone we can call for you, or we can take you home? You said you don't live far. What is your address?" The rapid fire of the questions frazzled Ivy Lee even more. Her eyes were blank as the repeated questions resounded in her ears.

"I don't know. My husband, Willie drives me everywhere." Ivy Lee cried. The two decided they would take her to the police station in hopes someone would search for her.

"I know my telephone number, but my Willie wouldn't be home yet. My number is TY5-4664."

Ivy Lee shivered, as the taller police officer led her to the police car. Although she was getting in the back of a police car, she felt safer. The gas station attendant kept staring at her, or at least she imagined he was. They arrived at the police station, and as they pulled up, she noticed what she thought was Willie's car. As they headed towards the door, Willie was leaving and called to Ivy Lee as he rushed towards her.

"Ivy Lee!! Thank God! I've been searching all around the neighborhood for you. I'm glad you're safe." He pivoted to the officers, thanking them.

"Sir, may I have your name?" said the shorter officer addressing Willie.

"My name is Willie Patterson, I'm her husband." He pulled Ivy Lee closer to him.

"We found your wife at the gas station, at the corner of Livernois and Davison. She seemed disoriented."

"Ivy Lee, you came all this way. Where were you going? It's dark out. Please don't do this again." Willie said with both fear and concern in his voice.

She sheepishly buried her head in Willie's chest and stayed silent. The two officers gave a nod to Willie to take Ivy Lee home.

Chapter 26

Confidant

Ivy Lee was quiet for the rest of the week. Willie was overly attentive and stayed close to home declining any extra church duties. Ivy Lee assured him she wouldn't venture out of the house. Willie complied with Ivy Lee's request. He didn't tell her about the incident.

Ivy Lee called Ida Mae and invited her for a visit. They enjoyed each other's company. Ida Mae was excited and said she would bring over a lemon pound cake from a new recipe she was eager to try.

Ivy Lee woke early to make Willie breakfast. He made sure she took her morning dose of medicine. She expected Ida Mae to arrive around noon. She baked a homemade chicken pot pie from one of Tommie's favorite recipes. Ida Mae arrived around noon. They enjoyed lunch followed by tea and pound cake while watching soap operas.

"Ivy Lee, I'm so glad you asked me to come over. I have missed you, and we have a good time."

"Me too. I've been down lately. Can I tell you something? I can't confide in anybody else. I trust you, Ida Mae."

Ida Mae put down her cup and took Ivy Lee's hand. "Yes, of course you can trust me."

Ivy Lee spoke deliberately. "I ventured out to the store last week and got lost. The police took me to the station, where Willie was waiting. Something else happened. I think I let someone in the house. I know it wasn't a dream, because I found a watch in the living room, and it doesn't belong to Willie." Tears streamed down Ivy Lee's face. Her almond-shaped eyes widened, and in a hoarse whisper, "I think I slept with him. I only remember waking up naked, scared, and then finding the watch."

"Oh no Ivy Lee! Do you think he attacked you?" Ida Mae scooted closer and hugged Ivy Lee.

"No, but I don't know why it happened." She broke down. "I don't know why! When I have spells, I keep waking up in the basement. It brings back terrible memories from my childhood."

"It's ok, Ivy Lee, it's ok." Ida Mae concerned about her cousin pacified her until she calmed down. She spent the next hour listening to Ivy Lee's recollection of her experience and assured her things would get better and encouraged her to seek therapy again. Ivy Lee didn't mention the usher, but felt much better having someone to confide in. Something she could never do with Mabel.

On Ida Mae's encouragement, Ivy Lee pursued treatment which finally seemed to work. She took her medicine regularly, suffered fewer lapses, managed her triggers, and agreed to go in for extended treatment, when necessary, which turned out to be less frequent than in the past. Feeling somewhat normal since she first acknowledged her symptoms, she was optimistic about her relationship with Willie. She felt renewed and relaxed.

Chapter 27

Graduation

The years passed by so swiftly. Ivy Lee couldn't believe Riley was all grown up. Mabel, Randall, Willie, and Ivy Lee beamed as he walked across the stage at his graduation ceremony. The rest of the summer was bittersweet. Riley signed up to join the U.S. Air Force and was leaving the September after graduation.

The four of them accompanied him to the airport. Riley hugged Mabel extra-long and assured her as soon as he got out of basic training, he would make his way home for a visit. His assurance did little to comfort her, but she knew she needed to let him pursue his dream. He wanted to be a pilot since he was a young boy. Both Mabel and Ivy Lee shared stories about his uncle Frank's pursuit of being a pilot. He hugged Ivy Lee as she held back tears. As they watched the plane depart, Ivy Lee felt a renewed sense of loss, but tried to conceal it and hold on to the memories of the time she and Riley spent together. Mabel and Ivy Lee locked arms as they leaned on each other on their way to the car as Willie and Randall followed.

Chapter 28

Christmas

The beautifully decorated Christmas tree practically reached the ceiling. Ivy Lee gradually added decorations over the past week. She planned to have people over from the church on Christmas Eve to sing Christmas carols. She invited Aunt Lillian and Uncle Ben. Lillian was so nice to her when she lived in the upstairs flat above Mabel. Ida Mae arrived first and helped Ivy Lee put the finishing touches on the place settings. Lillian arrived alone since her husband Uncle Ben's' arthritis flared up.

The buffet held all kinds of Christmas cookies, eggnog, and appetizers. Ivy Lee took a moment to soak in the scene. She was happy everything worked out. Ivy Lee was a gracious host who went around serving appetizers and made sure everyone enjoyed themselves. The chiming of the doorbell was a surprise since all the invited guests arrived. Willie shouted and let Ivy Lee know he'd answer the door, as she joined the group to begin another song.

The cold draft from the open door made Ivy Lee turn towards it. It stunned her to see Willie helping Mabel with her coat since she didn't invite her. It never dawned on her Mabel would be interested, since she was a Jehovah's Witness and never celebrated Christmas.

"Hi Sister! I'm surprised to see you. Did you come alone?"

"Yes, Ivy Lee, I'm by myself. Randall is home asleep. Lillian said you were having a party tonight. I guess I don't remember getting an invitation."

"Sorry Mabel, I didn't think you'd be interested, since it's a Christmas gathering, but you know you're welcome here anytime." She reached out to welcome her with a hug.

"Well, it sure didn't feel like it! I'm your sister!" Mabel went over to peruse the buffet. Ida Mae immediately came over to Ivy Lee, as she could see Mabel's arrival affected her cheerful demeanor.

"Are you ok?" Ida Mae touched Ivy Lee's arm.

"I didn't invite her. She just showed up. I hope she doesn't cause any problems. She doesn't get along with Aunt Lillian. I wanted to have a peaceful gathering."

Ivy Lee busied herself in the kitchen by filling trays and bringing out more appetizers. As she entered the living room, she noticed Mabel having a heated exchange with Aunt Lillian. Everyone else seemed to be oblivious to their conversation, and Ivy Lee watched as if in slow motion. Mabel stood holding a plate of food and Aunt Lillian seemed to be agitated. Aunt Lillian stood up, practically toe to toe leaning in close to Mabel.

"Let me tell you something, Miss Mabel, maybe you can boss Ivy Lee around like a little child, but I'm not your sister, and I won't stand for it. You stroll around like you're so perfect, but I haven't forgotten the past. Don't make me air all your dirty laundry here, cause I will. You don't want to tangle with me." Aunt Lillian stepped around Mabel intentionally brushing her shoulder as she went in the kitchen to replenish her plate. The raised tone of Aunt Lillian's voice caused everyone to pause momentarily, but Ida Mae distracted them by starting another song. Willie came over to Ivy Lee to check on her. She kept her eyes on Mabel, who entered the kitchen where Aunt Lillian was by the stove.

"Let me tell you something, I don't have secrets, or nothing to hide. I'm not perfect, but I'm no monster either, so don't you threaten me!" Mabel stood waiting on a response, a hand on her hip, and the other holding her plate.

Aunt Lillian came up close whispering in Mabel's ear. "I don't pretend to know all the details of Riley's adoption, but I bet there was deception on your part. I wouldn't trust you with a dog, and like I told you many moons ago, stay away from me and mine. Jehovah Witness or not, you ain't changed much." She glowered at Mabel then went to the living room and approached Ivy Lee, quickly changing her disposition.

"Ivy Lee don't worry. Mabel and I spoke. I would never disrupt your lovely party. Everything is beautiful, and the food is delicious. Thank you for inviting me."

"Thank you, Aunt Lillian. I'm so glad you could make it, and I hope Uncle Ben feels better. Please fix him a plate." Ivy Lee announced as she went to find Mabel, who sat at the dining room table alone. She appeared annoyed but continued eating her food.

"Mabel, is everything, all right?" Ivy Lee said sitting down in the chair next to Mabel.

"You invited the old goat, didn't you? I'm your sister, and you didn't even invite me." Mabel said with disgust.

"Well, I know you don't celebrate Christmas, so it's the only reason I didn't include you. Aunt Lillian has been kind to me. I don't know what happened between you, but I hope you two can makeup someday."

"You better watch out for her. I have known her for many years, and she likes to spew lies about me. She's related by marriage, but she ain't blood! I don't trust her, and you shouldn't either."

"She has said nothing to me about you. Is there anything I can get you?

"No, I'm fine. This is a beautiful party."

"Thank you. It's my favorite holiday." Ivy Lee returned to her guests and took the lead on the next Christmas carol, her favorite, *Oh Come All Ye Faithful*.

The night ended quietly. Plenty of leftovers remained and Ivy Lee assisted by Ida Mae packed them for the guests.

She reminisced about the Christmases with Riley. Those years passed by quickly. Her poor recall of the events of Riley's birth contributed to her heartbreak. She couldn't be certain about the arrangement because of her illness. She hoped there wasn't anything dishonest in the process but continued to mourn the time she'd lost. She learned to hide her sadness, through her involvement with the church, but the grief remained and surfaced in her quiet times.

Willie escorted Mabel to her car, who quietly exited after giving Ivy Lee a brief hug. Ivy Lee was happy with the outcome. Willie helped her with the dishes and put away the remaining food. She was relieved Mabel and Lillian's behavior didn't get out of hand. She knew they shared history, but neither of them divulged the details, so she never knew what the tension was between them.

Chapter 29

Riley Visits Northlawn

It was the end of 1969. Ivy Lee relapsed many times over the last five years. She woke up surrounded by ambiguous faces, unable to focus in on any of them. The first silhouette was tall; the height of the images appeared to descend like stairs. She recognized Riley's face, or at least she thought it was him. Since Riley was in the Air Force and stationed in Texas, it was a few years since she saw him. He now had a full mustache and a muscular frame.

"Aunt Ivy Lee! It's me Riley!"

"Riley! Oh Riley! I'm so pleased to see you! I'm so sorry you must see me in here! She said as her voice choked up.

"Please don't cry. We're happy to see you. We're in town for a couple of weeks." Ivy Lee's sight focused on a woman holding a child.

"Auntie, meet my family. This is my wife, Sheila. Debra is the oldest, then Vincent, and Ryan is the baby."

"What a lovely family Riley. I'm so proud of you."

"Thank you. We can't stay long. Mom is having dinner and told us to be back by four o'clock. We'll be back to visit before we leave town. We are thinking about moving back when I'm discharged. We've been looking for houses." Riley came over and hugged Ivy Lee. "I've missed you so much, Auntie."

"I love and miss you so much Riley. I've been so lonely since Willie passed. His death shattered me. I stopped taking my medicine and relapsed. I miss him so much and still can't believe he's gone."

Willie never was a great sleeper and worried about Ivy Lee.

"The police think he fell asleep driving home from work. It was raining, and he went off the road."

A tear trickled down Ivy Lee's face, as she leaned against her bed. Riley came over and held her until she seemed to calm down while his young family watched.

"I know, I miss his hearty laugh. He taught me so much."

His embrace seemed to assuage her. He motioned to the children to come to Ivy Lee's bed side.

"Debra and Vincent, come over and give your Great Auntie a kiss." The children cautiously came over as Ivy Lee's face lit up.

"Sheila the little one looks like Riley when he was a baby."

"Yes, I agree. Mabel showed me those pictures. They look like twins!" said Sheila as she kissed Ivy Lee on the cheek and held a sleeping Ryan up close so Ivy Lee could kiss him.

Their visit lifted her spirits. She watched them file out of her room, She couldn't believe Riley was a grown man with a family, but she was ecstatic he was moving back to Detroit.

***

The darkness returned before too long. Ivy Lee felt alone, and an immense sadness covered her. They gave her sedatives to sleep because she paced all night calling out for Willie and Georgia. When pressed to spend time in the community room, she stared out the window. One woman who stayed in a corner kept banging her head on a wall. Other patients appeared comatose; some screaming, rocking back and forth, and others remained quiet. She kept to herself.

She lost track of the time she remained in the facility; every day was a blur. She dreaded going to sleep at night because sometimes she felt like someone was hovering over her and trying to touch her. Once she awakened to what she thought was a dark figure fleeing her room. She couldn't discern whether it was real or a dream.

Mabel visited once a week, bringing clean clothes, and books and magazines to read. Their conversations were typically sparse. They were both widows now; Randall died suddenly a year before. Mabel got the call to come to the shop because he'd collapsed. She made it there as the ambulance attendants attempted to revive him, but to no avail. It was a massive heart attack. Mabel noticed his ashen face and his eyes rolled back when she arrived and knew he was gone. She made all the workers leave and padlocked the collision shop, in fear his tools and equipment would disappear. Randall regularly hired several men from the neighborhood; Mabel told him to be careful. She sold the shop within a few months along with his boat but gave all his fishing rods and his tackle box to his best friend, Larry.

Mabel dreaded every time Ivy Lee asked about Georgia. She continued to give the same answer; she was their baby sister buried in Wadesboro. Ivy Lee kept asking, how she died, but Mabel said she didn't know. This inquiry came up during each visit.

Ivy Lee's condition improved slowly, calmer and less agitated, but short lived. Mabel didn't know what to expect with each visit. The doctor said they would release her over the next month. Mabel helped Ivy Lee sell the house after Willie died. She knew Ivy Lee wouldn't be able to live on her own, and it was good the upstairs flat was vacant. She welcomed the company. Between Randall's sudden death and Riley living out of state for now, she felt isolated. She needed Ivy Lee as much as Ivy Lee needed her, but a call from Dr. Timmons relayed the news of another relapse, which postponed her release. It was an unexpected setback.

Chapter 30

Ivy Lee Rebounds

Ivy Lee felt like she'd been in a thick fog. She knew Dr. Timmons wouldn't release her in this state. She reverted to the moment the police arrived at her door and informed her of Willie's death. The deep dark sadness returned. She felt like she was in a dark hole; she could see light, but when she tried to climb to the top, she sank deeper in darkness.

Dr. Timmons tried changing her medicine over the last two months. She sat and stared at the wall all day. She waited for sundown and sunrise. Dreary days were the worst. Although she used to love thunderstorms and rain, she found herself crouched in the corner. She faintly remembered Mabel's visits, although she felt her presence when she was there. Her voice sounded muffled, and when she tried to speak, nothing came out, and she cried. Dr. Timmons mentioned an experimental electroshock treatment, but she didn't even know what it meant, and she was afraid to think about it. She saw Dr. Timmons speaking with Mabel, but she couldn't hear what they were saying.

On the morning of her first ECT procedure, Ivy Lee remembers being hungry since not allowed to eat before the procedure. Dr. Timmons explained she would be sedated and a light electric shock administered to her brain. He assured her the procedure was painless. Nurse Emily accompanied her and was there when she woke after the procedure. They wheeled her on a gurney into a cold gray room with bright lights. One arm wrapped with a blood pressure cuff, while the puncture of the needle for anesthesia in her other arm. Nurse Emily placed the bite guard in her mouth and coached her to relax. She remembered feeling woozy as she awoke in a room with other patients, and being offered food. As Nurse Emily wheeled her to a ward with three other women, she hesitated and stared at the nurse.

"This is not my room. Where am I?" she said gripping the arms of the wheelchair.

"This is temporary, Mrs. Patterson. You will spend a few hours here to be monitored after your procedure." She tried to convince Ivy Lee. Ivy Lee surveyed the room, and each of the women were quiet, two seemed to be asleep, with their backs facing her, one snoring loudly, her wrinkled gown scarcely covering her large frame revealing her large, dimpled buttocks, and the thin gray-haired elderly woman who held her knees to her chest while rocking and mumbling.

As Ivy Lee rose from the wheelchair, her head was pounding, Nurse Emily guided her to the bed. She woke up the next morning back in her room her head still shrouded in fog. She spoke with Dr. Timmons shortly thereafter, but struggled to remember the treatment, the first of many which seemed to fortify her.

As the sun came up, Ivy Lee could feel the warmth on her face. It felt good; It felt good to feel something. The nurse came in with her tray, and she felt hunger pangs when she smelled the food. She gave Ivy Lee her morning meds and Ivy Lee asked her if she could sit in the chair and eat. She obliged Ivy Lee with a smile and moved the tray over to the seat near the window in the corner.

"You seem better Mrs. Patterson, how do you feel? The new treatment seems to have helped you."

"I'm hungry, and I feel like taking a shower. Can I take a shower?"

"Of course, you can. I'm so glad you are feeling up to it. I'll be back in about a half hour to assist you."

"May I have a brush and comb; I would like to braid my hair?"

"Absolutely! So glad to see you up. I will update Dr. Timmons. Your sister has been asking to come and visit you. Are you up to it?

The last few times, you have refused her visits. It's been a month since she's been here."

"Yes! I want to see my sister. Please call her."

Ivy Lee ate her breakfast, showered, combed her hair, and put on fresh clothes. She sat in the armchair in the corner, picking up her Bible from the windowsill and flipped to her favorite scripture, Psalms 23. Reading every word of the verse she said a silent prayer thanking God for everything. As she closed the Bible, she hummed her favorite hymnal, *Blessed Assurance*. This song brought her joy.

Ivy Lee felt refreshed. Her reflection in the mirror revealed the gauntness in her eyes, and excessive weight loss. For the first time, she noticed the gray hair at her temples. She smiled thinking about Tommie's sprinkles of gray at her temples as a young Mother, and how pretty the silver shimmers were. Mabel said she would never let her hair turn gray and dyed it at the first peek of gray from her roots.

Ivy Lee opened the top drawer of the dresser and saw her tattered notebook. This was her cherished book of poems. She flipped through the pages until she landed on a poem she wrote after her return from Raleigh. It brought back fond memories.

Lilac Tree

I'm like the Lilac Tree,
just basking in the shade
Shyly blooming all my buds,
and releasing a sweet bouquet
No one even notices me,
as I mingle among the crowd.
But their senses can't ignore,
my intoxicating invisible cloud.
Beautifully part of the background,
But drawing subtle attention my way
lavender flowers waft with the breeze
While my branches slightly sway
Yes, I'm like a Lilac Tree, beautiful,
delicate, and, free
Waiting for my Southern Knight to
come and rescue me.

Chapter 31

Sisters Reunited

Ivy Lee's s skin savored the warmth as she faces the window for the first time in months. She recognized she lost track of time and couldn't remember the last time she had left her hospital room. She was too paranoid. The leaves announced a change in the season since her admission, changing color from a green hue until turning brown. Fall was her favorite season, but she missed it while in the hospital. The change in the weather and the falling leaves, brought back memories of visits to the cider mill which used to bring her joy.

Ivy Lee spent a full year in Northlawn Hospital. Mabel arrived at 10 o'clock and signed the release papers. Her life was changing, and she was nervous. She and Ivy Lee would share the same space again. Ivy Lee would live in the upstairs flat. She regretted the way she treated Ivy Lee, but it was clear the two widows genuinely needed each other.

She turned around as she heard Mabel opening the heavy metal door. She wore her short sleeved blue dress, her favorite color.

"Good morning, Ivy Lee! Are you ready to go home?"

"Yes! I just want to be normal again. I've heard and seen things that make me sad."

"I'm glad you're coming home. You're doing so much better. I hope you don't have to return here. I'm happy for you Sister."

Mabel embraced Ivy Lee in a prolonged hug. Ivy Lee waited for this moment and hoped it would last. Mabel seemed different to her now; somewhat diminished, and she seemed to have aged. The times were few when she witnessed Mabel being kind. Since Mabel lost Randall, it seemed to have changed her disposition considerably.

Ivy Lee asked if they could take a drive around Belle Isle Park. She and Willie used to spend hours out there. Their favorite spot was under a willow tree where they watched the cargo ships go up and down the Detroit River on the Detroit side which overlooked the Windsor, Ontario shoreline. Willie promised to take Ivy Lee to Canada, but between frequent trips to the hospital, they never found the time.

Willie hoped for a more normal life with Ivy Lee each time they discharged her from the hospital. Sometimes she needed to go back; a repetitive cycle which he endured for several years.

Mabel decorated the upstairs flat with furnishings from Ivy Lee and Willie's home. Ivy Lee was so happy to see it and thanked her profusely.

"Mabel, this feels like my home. I've loved this flat, and you've made it beautiful."

Ivy Lee stepped out on the upstairs porch and surveyed the neighborhood. It brought back bittersweet memories of Willie trimming the shrubs.

After she put away her few belongings, she went out on the upstairs back porch which overlooked the brick barbeque pit, the grape vines, and the plum tree. This scene brought back additional memories of family gatherings.

Mabel invited Ivy Lee downstairs for dinner, which gave her several hours to reorganize a few of her belongings and rest. She swallowed her medicine and lay down for a brief nap before dinner. She had little appetite while taking the medicine, one of the side effects Dr. Timmons mentioned, but she knew she should eat.

Chapter 32

Epiphany

"I wanted to make our first dinner together special. Would you like to make the salad? Tomatoes and cucumbers are in the refrigerator. The crystal salad bowl is in the cabinet to your left."

"I would be glad to!" said an excited Ivy Lee.

Mabel stirred the fresh lemonade, while Ivy Lee peeled and tore each leaf off the head of lettuce for the tossed salad. Ivy Lee thought Mabel was a little distracted, and unusually quiet, and she hoped the evening would be pleasant.

"Well, Ivy Lee. Everything is ready, let's eat."

Ivy Lee carried the salad and followed Mabel into the dining room. There was a lemon meringue pie on the buffet.

"The pie looks delicious, Mabel."

"I knew it used to be one of your favorites. I haven't made one in years."

They made polite conversation as they ate. Ivy Lee noticed Mabel subdued, nervous, and a little sad.

"Mabel, are you alright? Did I do something wrong?"

"No Ivy Lee, everything is ok. When we're done with dinner, let's chat in the living room. It won't take long to clean up the dishes. I'll wash, and you can dry, ok?"

"I'm happy to do it. Everything was delicious!"

They finished up the dishes, wiped the counters and Ivy Lee swept the floor. It seemed like old times to Ivy Lee, except this time,

Mabel was not ordering Ivy Lee to do it. Ivy Lee sat on the sofa while Mabel sat in a corner chair with the pole lamp with little shades hanging over it.

"This pie is good!"

"I'm glad you like it. Would you like some tea?"

"No, I'm fine. I'll put this in the sink."

Ivy Lee came back to the living room and sat down facing Mabel. Mabel nervously faced Ivy Lee and appeared to be hesitant to speak.

"Ivy Lee, I love you and I'm glad you're here. I'm happy we have each other, but I must tell you something."

"Yes, Sister. Tell me." Ivy Lee braced herself.

"I know you have been having dreams about Georgia. Do you remember what happened?" Mabel asked.

"Yes, I think I understand now, and it makes me sad. I didn't mean to hurt her." Ivy Lee's voice choking up.

"Please don't get upset. It was an accident, and I'm so sorry I blamed you. I was glad you didn't remember. You loved Georgia and took such good care of her. Do you remember when Mama sent me to Tampa after I broke up with Ozias to visit our cousins before Georgia was born?"

"Yes, I remember. You must have liked him a lot. I remember you were sad."

Mabel let out a sigh and paused. "Mama sent me away because I was pregnant."

"Pregnant? Oh no! What happened to your baby?" Ivy Lee asked. Tears fell from Mabel's eyes. Ivy Lee got up and went over to Mabel to comfort her.

"Baby Georgia, baby Georgia, she was my daughter."

Ivy Lee stunned; unable to move or speak. She felt like she was right back in the muddy field, but she remembered the therapy with Dr. Timmons and closed her eyes and inhaled deeply. Mabel, sobbed uncontrollably, and Ivy Lee took her hands in hers, as her own tears fell.

"Mabel, I understand now why you were so protective of her. I'm so sorry," She put her head on Mabel's lap.

"Ivy Lee, I know, it was an accident and I forgive you, and I want you to forgive yourself. I carried the burden of your truth to protect you."

"Thank you, Mabel. I loved Georgia."

"Do you remember seeing Ozias and the Johnsons at Georgia's graveside?

"Yes. It was strange that he was there."

"Ozias was Georgia's father. Her hazel eyes were just like his."

Ivy Lee and Mabel hugged and cried for what seemed like hours. Eventually, Mabel got up and made them both teas. The night ended with them both red-eyed and exhausted. Ivy Lee retreated upstairs, sleeping better than she had in a while. She felt lighter emotionally and physically; a great weight lifted.

Chapter 33

Riley

The bald tires squealed as Mabel swiftly pulled into the parking space behind the blinking red lights of the ambulance. She flung the car door open and ran up the wooden porch stairs all but tripping when she reached the top step. She threw open the screen door as the medic finished strapping Riley on the gurney.

"Ma'am please move! We must get him to the hospital." The taller medic said. His face was red and sweat glistened on his forehead.

"What happened to my Riley? She screamed. Turning towards Sheila, Riley's wife, who was shielding three small children behind her.

"Miss Mabel, I mean Mom, I couldn't wake him up."

Mabel and Sheila didn't have a good relationship. She criticized Sheila's, housekeeping, cooking, and even the way she took care of the kids. She told Sheila she wasn't good enough.

"You trapped my son." She remembers Mabel saying when she found out Sheila was pregnant with their first child before they got married.

"Can you watch the kids? I need to ride in the ambulance." Mabel nodded.

"Ma'am hurry!" She heard the taller medic scream as the siren blared, grabbed her purse, and raced down the steps.

As Sheila leaned back in the firm yellow upholstered low back sofa, she stared down at her feet and saw her mismatched house slippers. One was a blue one, with flowers across the top, and the other a pink one coming apart at its sole. For a moment she felt

127

embarrassed, but she was more worried about her Riley. She tried to push her emotions about Mabel to the side, but imagined her going through the house and critiquing everything.

"Family of Riley Jackson?" The gray-haired doctor shouted as he opened the double doors of the emergency waiting room.

"Yes, I'm Mr. Jackson's wife." Sheila inched across the waiting room to meet him and hoped he wouldn't notice her shoes. Dr. Lane pulled her over to a quiet corner of the waiting room where they sat down. The frigid air conditioning in the waiting room gave her a shiver which added to her nervous state.

"How is Riley?" she said with trepidation in her voice.

"We don't know yet. He came in with a weak pulse, severely dehydrated, and we are monitoring his kidneys. We have started an I.V. but he has shown little response; he remains unconscious. We are waiting on the result of the bloodwork." Sheila felt weak, and Dr. Lane held her hand to calm her.

" I will send the nurse out when you can see him." He patted her hand to assure her.

"Thank you." She found it hard to speak with the lump in her throat, as she watched his white coat disappear through the swinging double doors.

A couple of hours passed in the waiting room and Sheila woke up to realize the sun already set.

I need to call home. She thought.

A cheerful young nurse led her back to see Riley. He was still unconscious and pale. Dr. Lane entered and Sheila noticed his tall frame.

"Well, we do have some answers. It appears from the bloodwork; his blood sugar is extremely high, and it has left him in a in a diabetic coma."

"I don't understand." She said as her eyes widened.

Dr. Lane handed Sheila a pamphlet which helped explain Riley's condition. He told her if Riley regained consciousness, he would need a drug called insulin and he must change his diet. Sheila prayed silently as Dr. Lane answered a few more of her questions and swiftly exited after being paged on the intercom.

The green Checker taxicab pulled in the neighbor's driveway next door to drop Sheila off. The porch light illuminated the walkway as she quietly put the key in the door and crept upstairs, passing Mabel on the couch who was sound asleep and snoring loudly. Sheila had never witnessed Mabel at this level of agitation before. She brushed it off as concern for her only child.

The next morning, when Sheila entered Riley's room, he was conscious and sitting up. Released two weeks later, her prayers answered. It took him some time before he regained his strength to return to work. Dr. Lane assured him he thoroughly filled out the required paperwork to keep his job. They were relieved his employer agreed to hold his job on the assembly line. Riley returned to work adjusting to his new way of eating and insulin shots. He watched Sheila's hands trembling, as she practiced sticking a syringe into an orange to learn how to administer an insulin shot.

Chapter 34

Mabel

"Hello! Sheila!" Riley screamed into the telephone.

"Riley! What's wrong?"

"Mom suffered a stroke, I'm at the hospital. She can't feel her left side or speak right now, but they say it may return."

"Riley, I'm so sorry. How can I help? Riley? Riley?"

Muffled sobs emanated from the other end of the telephone. She continued calling his name.

"I'm here, sorry. I love Mom so much." His voice cracking. "I will call you back. The doctor is here." He hung up abruptly. Sheila held the telephone for a moment before hanging up the receiver. She never heard Riley so upset; it was the first time she ever heard him cry.

After receiving an update from the doctor, Riley felt calmer. The test results were promising. He spun around as the husky sound of Mabel's voice startled him.

"Riley? I need to talk to you. Come closer baby."

"Mom, it's so good to hear your voice, but don't speak. Get some rest. I spoke to the doctor. You suffered a stroke, but it seems to be a mild one. Can you move your arm?"

"No, I've tried. I feel a tingling, but it feels heavy. Please pull up a chair. I need to tell you something."

Riley pulled the chair in the corner closer to the edge of Mabel's bed. She reached out to Riley with her trembling right hand and grabbed his forearm as a bulge formed in her throat making it difficult for her to speak. She swallowed and asked Riley to get her a sip of water, which he obliged her with the cup on her tray.

"I don't know where to begin." She said in a strained voice. "A long time ago when you were a baby, we made an important decision." She paused. "I love you. It has not, and will never change."

"Mother, I don't understand. Of course, I know you love me. What decision? I am confused. You need to rest. Let's discuss it when you get home."

"No Riley, please listen to me. The short time I couldn't speak terrified me. I thought I couldn't tell you this. Please don't be mad with me. I now realize it was wrong to keep this from you."

"Don't worry. I love you. I could never be upset with you."

"Riley, I.., I, I am your Mother, but I am not the Mother who gave birth to you. You have been mine from the first days of your birth."

"Mother, I don't understand. What do you mean, you are not my Mother? You are my Mother!"

"Your birth Mother was sick, mentally sick. She could not take care of you, so I stepped in. I adopted you and later, Randall adopted you and gave you his family name." Riley took a deep breath. The news was overwhelming. He forgot he was in the hospital.

"Why are you telling me this now? You are my Mother!" His booming voice filled the room.

"Riley, I didn't want something to happen to me without you knowing the truth."

"The truth? I understand, but you need to rest." He leaned over to kiss her on the forehead.

"Your Aunt Ivy Lee is your birth Mother, Riley. Please don't be mad with her. She was a teenager when she became pregnant with you. She was not mentally stable to take care of you."

"Auntie is my Mother?" Riley's disposition changed to anger and more confusion.

"Yes. I'm sorry, but you need to know the truth."

"Why, Mother? Why now? His eyes filled with tears as he asked why he needed to know. I'll come back tomorrow." He said as he exited Mabel's room.

"Riley! Riley!" The nurse entered and ran over to Mabel's bed.

"Mrs. Jackson? Are you ok? Please try to calm down." Mabel didn't respond immediately, but tears streamed down her face. Lowering her head as a tear rolled down her cheek."I'm ok now."

Chapter 35

Houseguest

The day Sheila dreaded came to be. Her Mother-in-law, Mabel, was moving in. After her stroke, she couldn't live alone, at least temporarily or so Sheila hoped. Mabel's care was too much for Ivy Lee to handle. Ida Mae and other members agreed to check on Ivy Lee. Her behavior was more stable, but she still needed support.

Sheila noticed Riley avoided conversations about Mabel lately. It seemed to start before Mabel's release from the hospital. He said little about Mabel's condition other than she needed to move in. She could tell something was different about his demeanor. The way Riley and Mabel interacted appeared to be strained; they were usually close. Sheila kept asking him what was wrong, but he said everything was fine. She backed off. He wasn't distant with her before, and she never witnessed a void between him and Mabel. She queried Mabel, but Mabel said, Riley would share it with her when he was ready. Sheila found it odd; Mabel never missed an opportunity to interfere in their relationship before.

Chapter 36

Apogee

"Hello?"

"Auntie. How are you? May I come by?"

"Of course, Riley. I would love to see you. What time would you like to come?"

"Is noon too early?"

"Noon is fine. I'll see you then."

Ivy Lee was so thrilled not having seen Riley in a long time. She rushed into the kitchen to see what she could cook. It was a treat for her to cook for him.

In those few brief hours, Ivy Lee pulled together a full meal complete with homemade biscuits. She rested for a half hour, dozed off again, and then heard the doorbell.

"Riley!" Ivy Lee opened the door and reached out to give him a big hug, which he reciprocated and gave her a kiss on the cheek. Even though Riley was anxious, he couldn't turn down a delicious meal from his aunt. He was happy to accept the leftovers.

"Auntie, there is something I must ask you." He said in a serious tone.

"Riley, are you ok, is something wrong. You're not sick again are you. Have you been taking your insulin correctly?" Ivy Lee said in a worried tone.

"No, Auntie, don't worry. I'm fine. Let's sit down on the couch." Riley took Ivy Lee's hand. He wasn't sure how to approach the discussion, or how she'd react. He didn't want to trigger her, but he felt he needed to hear it directly from her.

"What is it baby? She said squeezing his hands in hers.

"Auntie when Mother was in the hospital and regained her speech, she said she needed to tell me something important."

"Yes, baby, what is it, is she sicker than she led on? Please tell me she'll be alright."

"No, it's not about her health. She explained when I was born, they took me from my Mother and said she is not my birth Mother. She said you, Auntie, are my birth Mother. Is it true?"

Ivy Lee hung her head and paused. "Yes, Riley, it's true, but listen to me. The treatments made me forget a lot about that time. The doctor thinks it's when my sickness first began. Riley, I couldn't take care of a baby; I couldn't take care of you. I'm so sorry and it doesn't mean I didn't want or love you. I knew Mabel would be a fine Mother. Sister and I agreed she would raise you as her child, and we would never tell you I'm your Mother. Over the years, I've regretted this decision many times. I've watched you as my nephew but loved you in my heart as my son. You deserved a Mother able to care for you and give you a good life. I was in no shape to give that to you. Can you ever forgive me?"

"Of course, I forgive you, Auntie. This is a lot of information. I didn't know, but I think I understand. You and I have a special connection. Can I ask another question?"

"Yes, Riley, anything." Ivy Lee's tears fell, but she felt relieved. Riley reached out and held Ivy Lee as she sobbed harder. Fresh tears covered his face. He held her for a while longer until it appeared she calmed down.

"Auntie, who is my father? Is he still alive?"

"I didn't tell anyone who your father is, not even my parents, and not Mabel. I was young, and he was quite older than me. His name is Samuel. I haven't heard from him since the summer I spent in Raleigh. I have a picture, but it's the only information I have about him. You see that picture over there of me holding a baby?" Riley nodded. "I have seen you stop by that picture many times. That was me holding you. I cried from afar as I ached to shower you with my love. It was difficult, but I was doing the best for you."

"Auntie, thank you. I know this is painful for you to share this with me. I love you, and my life has been great. Thank you so much for making my birthdays special each year. I looked forward to those cakes. You and Uncle Willie have been important to me. I know it must have been a hard decision, Auntie, but you weren't fully aware. You loved me enough to let me go ."

"Baby, I never wanted to disrupt your life. Mabel sent me pictures and kept me updated on everything going on with you from your first step to losing your first tooth while Willie and I were still in Jacksonville." Ivy Lee paused trying to assess Riley's emotions. "Are you ok, baby?"

"Yes, Auntie. This is a lot, but I have been avoiding my Mother since she told me the news. I was angry because I felt deceived; everyone else knew. I need to thank and reassure her, and most of all apologize. I feel bad for reacting like that. Now I understand why she was so protective of me. Thank you for the meal. I love you Auntie." He squeezed her tight, before coming back to the porch for another hug before he reached the car door.

Ivy Lee felt exhausted but relieved. She thought about calling Mabel and telling her about their conversation, but she thought it would be best not to intervene. She never interfered in their relationship. Although it was difficult, she stayed in the background because she knew it was better for Riley. The sisters agreed to never reveal it to Riley, and as hard as it was, she stayed silent. She could never have imagined Mabel telling Riley the truth. He was now aware, but it couldn't change the past.

Samuel was a distant memory since she never heard from him even after returning home. After sickness fell upon her after delivering Riley, she returned to Raleigh for a visit, but she doesn't think Aunt Debra and Uncle David were suspicious about her and Samuel.

After Riley left, she found the faded picture in her drawer of Samuel and Uncle David on their front porch in Raleigh. She never noticed Riley's gaped tooth smile mirrored the smile of Van, Uncle David, and Samuel.

Epilogue

It was six years since Riley returned to Detroit. He and his family moved to Texas shortly after both Mabel and Ivy Lee passed away two years apart; Ivy Lee succumbed to a heart attack, and Mabel from another stroke. He grieved losing the two most important women in his life and grappled with the circumstance of his birth. He embraced the reality and forgave all those who played a part once he accepted that the root of it all was based on their love for him.

As he drove through his old neighborhood, he reminisced about all the fun experienced while growing up, shooting marbles on the rubber runner on the front porch, and getting in trouble hanging around the railroad tracks. He thought about all the love from Randall, and Uncle Willie. He postponed this trip for years, but it pulled at his heart, and he knew what he needed to do to seek closure.

***

It was a hot day in mid-June, near Ivy Lee's birthday and several years since Riley's last visit to the cemetery. He pulled into the gravel lot to the cemetery office. The door chimes rang as they banged against the door. An older blonde-haired woman hunched over a typewriter looked up. Glasses perched on the tip of her nose connected by a thin chain around her neck, she returned a pleasant smile.

"May I help you?" she said as she stood up.

"Yes, I am trying to locate two plots. If my memory serves me correctly, I believe they are within a few feet of each other. The names are Mabel Jackson and Ivy Lee Patterson."

"Great. Have a seat while I check our card file." She slowly made her way to the wall of files with faded alphabets on each drawer. She appeared flustered and went back to her desk and appeared to be searching for something and stopped in front of her desk scratching her head, when it appeared what she searched for were her reading glasses around her neck. Her face flushed; she feverishly searched the index card file over the next ten minutes.

"I've found them both. Let me write the numbers on a piece of paper for you. It appears there is no headstone for either grave. You may need help in finding them. If you can't find them by the marker signs, wave down one of our attendants. They should be able to help you. Thanks for your patience." She handed Riley the two slips of paper.

"Thank you. Have a good day Ma'am."

"You too!" She shuffled back to her desk.

The searing sun was blazing as Riley followed the signs. Exasperated, he repeated his steps across the grass, being careful to avoid other plots. When he was about to give up, an attendant pulled up in his truck. The wheels caked with mud.

"Can I help you find a plot? I notice you've been searching for a while."

"Sure. I've tried. There are two of them." He handed the slips of paper over to the attendant who leaned back in the seat wiping his brow.

He held the paper up high. "Oh my, Barb's handwriting is hard to read, but I think you are near the right spot." He went back to his truck to grab a shovel. He put one muddy boot in front of the other appearing to measure the distance with his feet.

"Yep, they should be right here." He put his shovel in the dry grass while pressing his foot on the rusty shovel and applying his weight. He dug around, but seemed satisfied on the right spot. When he lifted the earth, it revealed a metal plot marker, the number barely visible.

"Ok, here is Mrs. Patterson, and Mrs. Jackson should be a few feet away." He again measured with his footsteps and when satisfied put the shovel in the ground, and appeared pleased with himself, as he uncovered the other plot marker.

"Here you go young man." Handing the paper back to Riley, he returned to his dusty truck.

"Thank you!" He stepped to the two holes which revealed the markers a few feet from one another. Memories of them washed over him. Each year, Uncle Willie, and Aunt Ivy Lee brought an Easter basket, and a carload of gifts at Christmas, even though they knew Mabel didn't celebrate the holidays. Tears filled his eyes. He suddenly remembered the two bouquets of flowers which lay on his back seat. He hoped the stifling heat didn't wilt them. He placed a bouquet down in each hole the cemetery attendant dug. He stood staring down and knew he needed a more permanent tribute to them. He remembered seeing the display of headstones near the entrance to the cemetery office. He got back in his car and headed back to the office. This time, his entrance appeared to have startled the clerk.

"Oh, hello there again. Did you have trouble finding the plots? I know my handwriting is terrible."

"No, your attendant found them for me. I am interested in purchasing headstones. Is it something you can help me with? I saw the display, but I wasn't sure you sold them here."

"Yes!! Let me get you the form." She handed him a pencil and shuffled through a stack of papers in her open desk file drawer. "Here you go! Fill them out and give them back to me. It takes about four to six weeks to complete it."

"Ok great." Riley sat down and carefully filled out the papers and handed the money to the clerk. She wrote him out a receipt on the carbon pad. "I will call you when they come in."

Riley left feeling less somber. He felt guilty for letting so much time lapse to carry out this task, but he was glad he accomplished it while he was in town. He wouldn't return to Detroit for a while. Accustomed to the warm weather in Texas, he hoped it was before winter set in.

It was over six weeks when he received a call from the cemetery notifying him of the delivery of the headstones. He scheduled his trip around Labor Day to make his way back to Detroit.

He drove to the area and found the section by himself. His stomach was uneasy as he stepped onto the gravel and made his way to their plots. His eyes widened as he admired the plots of the two women who showered him with immeasurable love. The headstones were virtually identical except the names, but they both read, "Loving Mother." Before he knew it, tears fell from his eyes, but the closure made him feel lighter.

I was fortunate to have the love of two mothers. He thought to himself as he pressed his fingers to his lips mimicking a kiss on each headstone pausing for a moment between the two and then headed back to his rental car to catch his flight home.